Arthur Ketchum, Herbert H. Lehman, Percival H Truman, Henry R
Conger

Williams Sketches

Arthur Ketchum, Herbert H. Lehman, Percival H Truman, Henry R Conger

Williams Sketches

ISBN/EAN: 9783337095826

Printed in Europe, USA, Canada, Australia, Japan

Cover: Foto ©Andreas Hilbeck / pixelio.de

More available books at **www.hansebooks.com**

WILLIAMS SKETCHES

BY

ARTHUR KETCHUM
PERCIVAL H. TRUMAN
HENRY R. CONGER

EDITED BY

HERBERT H. LEHMAN
ISAAC H. VROOMAN, Jr.

SECOND EDITION

WILLIAMSTOWN, MASS.
1898

ALBANY, N. Y.

JAMES B. LYON, PRINTER

TO

ALL WILLIAMS MEN

TABLE OF CONTENTS

PREFACE

TO begin a book by apologizing for it seems rather an undignified proceeding. Neverthless we have determined to preface these sketches with a few words of explanation.

When college stories have been written before it has always been by some alumnus. Now, the alumnus and the undergraduate look at college life from two very different points of view. The former has perspective and greater discrimination; his judgments in many respects are the more correct ones. But the undergraduate has the same advantage over him that the man in the street parade has over the person watching him from the sidewalk.

Preface.

College opinions and college problems are very vital matters to him, while they are dead issues to the older man. His views may be neither very mature nor very just, but at least they should be interesting as a study. If this book has any right to existence at all it is because it endeavors to present the undergraduate side of the question.

We are painfully aware of its immaturity, and are probably as much alive to its literary shortcomings as our most severe critics. But we shall be quite satisfied if those who read these stories find in them something which may serve to recall the half-forgotten memory of their life at Williams; that, supplementing our deficiencies by their own experience, they may look back with pleasure on the college that we all know and love.

THE BLACK SHEEP

The Black Sheep.

THE black sheep is the spice of the flock. It has long been held that no fold is complete without him. He has been held up as an example, and has done duty as a simile so long that he has gotten to hold a place among the literary "properties." As an animal, he has been misjudged and underrated; as an illustration, he is too useful to be eliminated. Sometimes the black sheep is not black at all, and, after he has been out in a kindly shower, comes back to his fellows as white as the rest. Sometimes he wanders far afield and gets lost on the hills — and sometimes he wanders again, and is led back to the fold with a blue ribbon about his neck.

This is how it happened once.

If you know anything about Williams you must know something about Billy Withers. Withers' power of getting himself talked about amounted to something like genius. Unfortunately, too. It is never pleasant to be fully aware that people are " onto " you,— especially when you are in college, and your doings are not always in accordance with the rules and precepts contained within the flimsy green covers of the Administrative Rules of the institution. At least, Withers did not care for the sensation. Sometimes the reports about him were grossly incorrect. Take, for instance, the time the Dean's dwelling was frescoed. Withers got all the blame, whereas, as a matter of fact, he had only suggested the scheme and superintended the decorations. And then, that memorable occasion when the pet donkey got into one of the instructor's class rooms. Why should Billy Withers have been responsible for that? Besides, as Bellew said, wasn't it just like a donkey to go to one of Sandy's lectures of its own free will? But all this, and much more, happened before Billy's senior year. There was not so much said of Withers and Withers' doings after that. Perhaps he had learned the gentle and useful art of covering his tracks. There was that silence about him which it might be well for Those in Authority to regard—and investigate—as suspicious. If they did, they could not have had the courage of

their suspicion; for they made no
sign, and the number of cuts against
Withers' name on the absence list,
posted in the hallway of Hopkins,
grew weekly more portentious.

It was one afternoon in early May
that Billy had to take a make-up for
one of Sandy's little exams. which he
had missed. He had just left the
room and was coming down the stairs
with the pleasing reflection, that, inas-
much as he had flunked the exam.,
there had been really no reason for
his having taken the trouble to climb
them, when Winthrop trotted down
after him and caught up with him.

"How did you hit it, Billy?" he
asked.

"I didn't touch it," said Withers,
"How'd you?"

Winthrop and Withers had roomed

together their freshman year. The bond formed from mutual Greek lessons and extra work troubles, however, did not seem strong enough to stand the separation of sophomore year, and they had lost each other. Besides, Withers had gotten an uncomfortable feeling once that Winthrop did not approve of him, and therefore, he had done the only thing possible in defense of his self-respect, and had disapproved of Winthrop.

So it came about that an occasional word and a passing nod was the whole story. Worthington Winthrop was a young gentleman whose morals were very much like his neckties,—always of the correct shape and never out of place. He always did his duty in an unenthusiastic, relentless way and was exasperating as an example. At least

Withers had thought so, whenever he had given the matter any consideration, but to-day, ——

Do you happen to know what mid-May is in Williamstown? When the great elms along Main street make deep caverns of shade for you to lie in and look out across sunny stretches of green lawn and terrace; with only the gleam of the white ducks of the men straggling out of a recitation in Hopkins, to divert your attention; and the tinkle of a mandolin drifting across to you through the Morgan ivies, or an echo of a song floating up from some where to weave into your dream — when the hills themselves· seem to have renewed their youth and grown sentimentally tender toward evening? Do you understand what it is to know all this, with the underlying remembrance that you are a senior, and are living and feeling, and being it all for the last time? Billy Withers did, as they came down the broad steps. There were some fellows on the lawn opposite playing ball, the strong afternoon sunlight bringing their white-clad figures out in clear-cut relief against the greenness.

Billy forgot that he had disapproved of Winthrop, or indeed, everything, except that it was good "to walk wi' man in fellowship." He lit a cigarette and put an arm over Winthrop's shoulder. "Where have you been keeping yourself for the last month?" he inquired, affably, "I've hardly seen you."

Winthrop refrained from turning the question back to the questioner. "Oh, I don't know," he answered, " fooling around, mostly. This last week I've been pretty busy, though; my mother and sister are staying here, you know."

" No ! are they ? I didn't know that," said Billy.

" Yes, they're going to be here right on through Commencement. By the way, they have been asking about you. They both want to see you." Winthrop put the last tentatively. It was as if he had said: " Will you come, or will you not ?"

Billy puffed for a moment in silence. It was odd how the mere mention of Winthrop's mother and sister's being in town raised that feeling of defiant recklessness. Billy himself had no mother, and Winthrop's, he remembered, was sweet and dignified and gracious, all that his ideal had always been. Billy remembered Winthrop's sister, too. He blew out another mouthful of smoke. "I shall be very glad to see them again," he said. "I have not had the chance since the Christmas vacation freshman year, I spent with you."

"Well, they haven't forgotten you," Winthrop said. "Let's see; they will be at home to-night. Can't you come up?"

Winthrop hesitated a second.

"I should be very happy to," he said.

"All right; they'll expect you then," and Winthrop went off across the lawn, whistling softly. When Billy got to his own room he threw himself down on his window bench and looked out into the quiet street. The sound of a cheer, softened by distance, came up from Weston Field. A little wind set the trees outside to whispering together. And Billy cursed himself for having been an ass, and fell asleep.

The Gym. clock had rung the hour and the quarter after when Sportie Bellew came up the stairs to Withers' door. As a warning of his approach he gave the door a kick, not because he wanted to announce his appearance, but he liked the noise. Bellew was the sort of a man who couldn't even breathe without making a fuss about it. He was a cheerful youth, withal, and of an infinite good nature. Billy Withers called him a " kid," but Bellew was a young person of experience. He came into Withers' room, and, standing in the middle of the floor, gazed at his host in silence. Then he went over and began piling up sofa cushions on the sleeping man's face. Withers brushed them off on to the floor, and, sitting up, winked in the light stupidly. "Oh, it's you, is it, Sportie?" he said, in a disappointed sleepy voice.

Bellew sat himself upon the desk. "Yes, it is I," he said. "And now, please tell me, where your college spirit is. Why aren't you down at practice instead of lying here asleep, and looking like a busted flush?"

"Make-up, in Sandy," Withers answered laconically.

"Hit it?"

"Flunked."

"Get out; you know you've had a drag with Sandy ever since you gave him thirteen reasons for divorce instead of the nine on the syllabus."

"I wish I thought so; but it doesn't

make much difference. I wouldn't have come back for it if it hadn't been for chapel."

"Pious boy! Have you seen the King to-day? Haven't you? Well, the Band of Mercy's going over to Stamford to-night."

Withers got up and crossing the room carefully straightened a picture before he spoke.

"Well, I am afraid the Band of Mercy will be without one of its brightest gems, then, because I can't be with you."

"You can't? Well, will you please tell me why?"

Withers studied the angle of the picture attentively.

"Because I've promised to call on Winthrop's mother and sister," he said.

His friend stared a moment.

"Well, I'll be damned," he remarked softly to himself.

Winthrop's people were staying at the Greylock. They had just come out from dinner when Worthington told his mother of Withers' coming.

"I am glad," she said. "What a nice boy he was. I wonder if he has fulfilled the possibilities of his face." Winthrop's mother was of the kind which young men of warm feeling and a limited vocabulary designate as "great." She was the sort of woman who could be motherly without appearing fussy, and who understood what questions not to ask. Winthrop adored her, and most of his friends followed suit.

"Elsie," said Mrs. Winthrop to her daughter, "will you find me my wrap?

I think I will go for a little walk in the park before it gets too dark."

The after-glow was dying in the west when they went out. Against the fleeting brightness the sharp cut hills seemed to have gained a new height and strange dignity. It was like a background that the early Italians painted behind some sweet-faced saint or the Madonna, Elsie Winthrop thought as she watched the color die, and the shadows, surging up through the cuts and ridges, grow cavernous and full of mystery.

Winthrop and his friend came across the little straggling park to find them just then, and together they all went back to where the lights of the big, barn-like hotel gleamed out through the deepening darkness.

When they came into the light of

the flaring gas jets, set at intervals along the broad piazzas, Withers, turning suddenly, met Mrs. Winthrop's eyes full on his face. The color mounted to the roots of his hair. "Oh, Mrs. Winthrop, you aren't going to tell me how much I've grown, are you?" he said, trying not to appear embarrassed. Mrs. Winthrop smiled.

"No, I can't tell you that, honestly, but you have changed," she said.

"College wouldn't amount to much if it did not change a man a little in four years," her son broke in.

Billy moved in his chair uneasily and began to talk about championship chances,— that safe conversational commonplace which is used so often in Williamstown that the usual observations on the weather almost acquire the dignity of epigrammatic originality.

17

There was an impersonality about the permutations and combinations of defeat and victory which should win or lose the pennant, that was grateful to Withers, and he explained the system to Elsie and Mrs. Winthrop with great exactness. It was easy to pass from base ball to other college topics, and the sound of the Gym. clock chiming the full hour came like a surprise to Billy, at least.

Winthrop stayed to say goodnight, and Billy went on down to his room alone. He lit a cigarette and pulled at it meditatively, as he walked slowly under the rustling arches that the elms made in the summer darkness over his head. "Mrs. Winthrop is a corker," he said, half aloud. "And what a nice little girl Winthrop's sister is! I had forgotten she was so pretty— no ; not that either exactly. She is more like the arbutus the fellows get in the spring. That's it."

There was a note stuck behind the card on Withers' door. Billy lit a match and read it while he was fumbling for his keys. It was brief and to the point.

"You're a quitter.

"(Signed) THE BAND OF MERCY."

It was in Bellew's handwriting, and Billy laughed and tore it up. Somehow he felt very respectable and decent. He even thought he would read Sandy's ten pages, and would have, if he had known where they began. He did not, however, so he took a cold bath instead, and then tumbled into bed.

Long after their visitor had gone

and her mother was asleep, Elsie Winthrop's light still burned. It was very late and the village street was dark and forsaken. The girl stood at her open window, looking out into the brooding night. There was a photograph in her hand and she was studying it intently. It was a picture of a young man with very much towsled hair and with a foot ball in his arms.

"He *has* changed," she said slowly at last, "mamma was right."

A sudden sound outside startled her. It was the noise of disordered singing. The men were driving evidently.

> "Here's to you Sportie Bellew,
>   Here's to you, our jovial friend,
>   And we'll drink to your health in this
>   God forsaken company,
>   We'll drink e'er we part
>   Here's to you Sportie Bellew."

They sang in inconsequent broken harmonies. The song grew fainter until the kindly silence received and hid it. Elsie held the little picture close to her.

"If he should be like that," she said in a frightened whisper, "I couldn't bear it."

Winthrop came over to Billy's room a day or so afterwards. He had hardly been in there since Billy had had it. Some of the things about gave a strangely familiar atmosphere to the place. The big brown photographs of the Landseer lions, with the fencing foils and masks stuck behind their frame, for instance; and the plaster cast of the pretty girl with the big hat and Parisian smile. Then Winthrop remembered that these same things had served to decorate the study that he and Withers had had in common. Billy was at the desk with his coat off, engaged in writing, when Winthrop entered.

"Be through in a minute," he said to Winthrop, "sit down."

There were other fellows lounging about the window seat and in the big chairs — Bellew and Hollins — "Didn't know Billy hung around with *him*," Winthrop thought — little Jack Ware of the Varsity and King Barnes.

Bellew had a mandolin and was trying to play "Tis with Love, true Love," from ear.

"For heaven's sake, Sportie, break away, I'm trying to write," growled his host, and the music stopped.

Presently the other fellows began to drop away with the unconventionality of great familiarity with the room and its owner, and Winthrop and Billy were left alone together. Billy brought the paper, on which he had been writing, down upon the blotter. "Thank the Lord that's through with," he said. "Have a pipe?" He filled his own carefully and lit it, puffing luxuriously. The two men sat talking idly of unimportant things until Winthrop got up and said he would have to be going.

"By the way," he said, as if he had just remembered it — although they both knew it had been the reason for his coming — "my mother wants to know if you will drive with us to the game to-morrow." It rather pleased Withers that they wanted him to be with them, and he accepted without any hesitation. If he had had time to think about it he would have refused, probably.

"Yes, he'll go," Winthrop told his mother later. "And we'll have to start early, because there's going to be a crowd."

"Worth," his sister said, "what is the Band of Mercy, or is that one of the things I oughtn't to ask about?"

"Where did you hear of the Band of Mercy?" asked Winthrop quickly.

"I saw it in the Gul. and was interested, because Mr. Withers' name was in the list."

"Oh, it's a sort of club," her brother answered — "a crowd of fellows, rather, who go together a good deal."

"Did you want to be in it?" inquired Elsie with sisterly directness.

Winthrop laughed.

"Under the circumstances, no," he said. "It's really not an organization anyhow, but merely a crowd of con-

24

genial fellows who trot about together and call themselves 'The Band of Mercy,' as a sort of joke. There are half a dozen or so of them; Barnes and Bellew —

"Bellew, Bellew?" Elsie broke in. Somehow the mention of the name had stirred a chord of memory. "Bellew — why, that is the name they were singing."

"Who were singing?" asked her brother.

"Oh, nothing; I was just trying to remember something," Elsie answered quickly.

When she was alone she sat down to think. "So those are his friends," she said; "those men who were drunk, and perhaps he, too, that very night, with them." And she hid her face in her hands. That was because she

25

was very young and a girl into the
bargain.

The game was a great success,— at
least from the Williams standpoint,
and after the crowd had cheered and
cheered again, they streamed up across
the field and over the old Campus to
the Morgan terrace for more cheering.

Elsie watched it all with great
excitement; it was very inspiring;
the cheers, the songs, the clanging of
the chapel bell; the crowds of hot but
enthusiastic "heelers," and she enjoyed it all. It gave Withers an odd
little thrill of pleasure when she asked
if this was the first game *we* had won.
She had puzzled him to-day; there
had come between them a sort of con-
straint and self-consciousness. Of
course, he could not explain it, nor
could Elsie either, only she was aware

that it was there. Withers thought of her as he went up to dinner. How pretty she was! He wondered why all girls didn't dress as she did. She wore awfully pretty dresses, Withers decided. And how different she was from all the others! The others—Withers thought of some of them and called himself a beast. Then he began to think of the game, and remembered again the twenty-five dollars he had won.

There was a special "Thanksgiving meeting" of the Band of Mercy that night. It was very long, and there was much business transacted. Billy Withers was there. Indeed, there is no telling how long he might have remained if King Barnes, just as the dawn was breaking, had not brought him home and put him to bed.

Of course, the next morning the usual occurred. It began when Withers, with a sick pain in the back of his head and dizzy eyes, staggered into his study from his bedroom and found there on the desk, where he had thrown it the night before, a crumpled, purple ribbon that she had worn. It deepened during the weary round of morning recitations. Sportie Bellew's facetious observations on the proceedings of the night before were not received amicably. The other fellows, seeing that he had a grouch, kindly left him alone.

Later in the afternoon Withers' meditations took shape and were put into action. He went up to the Grey-lock with a determination to tell her exactly what a beast he had made of himself; that he wasn't worthy to touch her hand; that he wanted her to give him another chance, and other confessions which would, no doubt, have been good for his soul, but were exceedingly hard to put into words. Unfortunately, there was a dapper little freshman calling on Miss Winthrop at the same time, and Billy's confessions had to be postponed. Perhaps the walk in the fresh spring air had done him good; at any rate, he was rather glad that the little freshman had been there, when he reflected on the matter as he walked back to the colleges.

There were a lot of seniors singing on the Morgan steps, but he did not care to join them. He saw Winthrop among them, and somehow he did not feel like having to talk to Winthrop just then.

Meanwhile Elsie had been coming to conclusions. Perhaps her brother had told her more than he had realized, in answering some of her questions.

To think with Elsie Winthrop was to act. But what could she do, she asked herself, in something like despair. There was no one to tell her what to do; it seemed almost hopeless. And yet she must do something. When she thought of the hero she had made of him for so long she wanted to laugh at herself, but even with the thought came a sense of triumph in the possibility of her helping him, " Even though he never knows," she told herself,— " or cares."

We play our parts in the human comedy so completely sometimes that we lose ourselves in them, and begin to think that we are no longer actors but masters of destiny. And then Fate pulls the strings, and we remember that we are only puppets after all, and must follow the stage directions.

Withers had grown inexplicable to his friends. The Band of Mercy frankly admitted that it was puzzled. " It's some confounded girl," said the gallant Hollins.

" Clever boy," Barnes answered. " How did you guess it? "

Hollins met Withers and Miss Winthrop on the Stone Hill road the next day, and began to see that Barnes had been sarcastic. When they reproached him with having shaken his old comrades, Billy only laughed and told them not to make that mistake.

The college year was drawing to an end. The senior exams. came, and

Billy Withers, to his own and every one else's surprise, passed them all. Maybe that was because Elsie read all her brother's careful notes to him and heard him go through yards of Sandy's syllabus, headings and sub-headings, points and by-points. The last days were bringing the little cliques of men closer together. It was almost pathetic to see how each one tried to get as much out of everything as possible.

The King and Bellew and Hollins were planning for a last blow out of the Band f Mercy. They were talking it over one morning on the Grey-lock piazza.

"It had better be to-night," the King said, "I'll telephone over now."

"Tell him we don't want American this time," said Bellew.

"Do you suppose that we can get Billy Withers? He ought to go if it's the last time," Hollins said.

At the sound of the name a pretty girl sitting next to him, put down the embroidery she was working with and leaned a little nearer.

"We'll make him. It can be his farewell performance, but he's got to go," the King said.

"What time do you start. Five?"

"Yes, its better to get over there early."

Elsie Winthrop's heart was beating quicker as she went into the hotel. She had decided on her course of action. It was for the last time as they said. But could she do it?

Withers found a note on his desk when he came back from lunch.

It read:

"DEAR BILLY.— I want to go up through the other glen this afternoon, to find maiden-hair. But I don't want to go alone. Will you not come with me? Besides, I want to see you about something. Come about four.

"Always yours faithfully,

"ELSIE COPE WINTHROP."

Barnes and Bellew came in just then and unfolded their plan for the evening.

"Of course you're with us, Billy," the King said.

"I don't believe —" Billy began.

Bellew interrupted: "Look here, Billy, it's the last time, you know, that we're going to be together. You aren't going to back out and spoil every thing at the very end of it all, are you?"

Withers looked out of the window

for a moment. It did seem like going back on them, and they had been his friends. Besides —

"What time do you start?" he asked.

"At five from Tom's," Bellew answered.

"If I'm not there at five don't wait for me," he said. And they parted.

It was a strange afternoon for Withers,— an afternoon of more serious thinking than he had ever known. It was a time when he spread out his whole life before his judgment, and calmly, coldly, almost, decided between the good and the evil in it,— the worth while and the worthless. He seemed to look into the face of all his possibilities, and he knew exactly where he stood. But the old habit clung; it is not so easy to relinquish one's pleasant lawlessness that the sacrifice does not bring a struggle. Which should it be? It was for him to choose which. And before he could decide it was four o'clock, and he was on his way to the Greylock. Though neither knew it of the other, each was passing through a strange and new phase of life that warm, still afternoon, up under the wood shadows. They talked of the little things about them, and if a deeper note was struck by chance, they both went back again to the old careless mood as if they dared not trust themselves. The light grew fainter and they turned homeward. Withers glanced at his watch as he walked; he could just get to Tom's on time if he hurried. For one mad moment he thought of leaving her there alone and run-

ning on to catch them before they
started.

Perhaps the other understood from
the look in his face what was passing
in his mind. She felt the time had
come.

"Do you remember," she said, trying not to appear conscious, "that vacation you spent with us? I shall
never forget it. You were the first
college man I had ever met, and somehow, of course it was absurd of me,
but I invested you with all the quali-
ties I had dreamed of. You were a
sort of hero, who couldn't do anything
evil or weak or unmanly —" her voice
trembled a little. "I was away at
school then, you know, and I used to
have your picture—a little kodak
Worth. took of you, in a purple
frame — there in my room. It was

foolish and young, of course, yet it can't be so bad for a man to have a girl's reverence and trust like that, can it?"

They were standing on a little hill through which the roadway made a sharp cut. As they stood there a three-seater passed beneath them. Some of the fellows in it looked up and, recognizing Withers, bowed.

"Who are they?" Elsie asked. Her heart was beating so she could hardly speak.

Withers watched the yellow carriage until it disappeared around a sudden turn.

"Oh, some fellows I knew once," he said slowly, after a pause.

And then he raised her hand to his lips and kissed it.

38

ODYSSEUS

39

Odysseus.

WHEN Perkins was a freshman, circumstances over which he had no control forced him into the society of Cecil Bancroft, the professor of the Greek language and literature. He not only met him with the rest of the class during the hours regularly devoted to the study of "Freshman Required," but on several occasions he was invited to be present at smaller and more select affairs, known to the initiated as "make ups."

However, Perkins was an affable individual, and he so conducted himself during his enforced attendance at these gatherings that they lost much of their

disagreeable character, and partook
more of the nature of informal Hel-
lenic afternoon receptions, with the re-
freshments omitted. One day, at the
close of a long conversation, which began with some remarks on the necessity
of his maintaining a better average in
Greek, and closed with the discussion
of a common friend, the principal of
Perkins' prep. school, the Professor
asked him to call; and the call was
the beginning of a very pleasant
friendship, which lasted during the re-
mainder of his college course.

After a while it became an understood thing that once or twice a term
Perkins should dine with the Professor; and he frequently, at the invitation of Mrs. Bancroft, attended faculty
teas; exciting affairs, where the professors' wives assembled and met to-

gether, apparently in order to discuss the difficulty of inducing competent cooks to remain in Williamstown.

It was during the winter term of his senior year that Perkins met the hero of this tale, and the circumstances of the meeting were as follows: He had been dining with the Professor, dinner was just over, and Perkins and his host were lighting cigars, at the urgent request of Mrs. Bancroft, who was one of those unselfish women who profess a fondness for tobacco smoke.

Suddenly something was heard scratching in the next room, and, when the door was opened, there entered a large black and white cat.

"Isn't this something new?" asked Perkins, "I don't remember seeing that cat before."

"Yes," answered Mrs. Bancroft,

"we've only had him a short time;
I must introduce you. Mr. Perkins,
may I present my friend, Odysseus?
Odysseus, this is Mr. Perkins."

"What a curious name for a cat,"
said Perkins, laughing. "How did you
happen to give it to him?"

"That is an idea of mine," explained
the Professor; "I call him Odysseus
because he is so seldom at home."

"He's a handsome beast at any rate,"
answered Perkins, and, stooping down,
he lifted the animal into his lap. Odysseus at first objected, but finally became reconciled to his position, and
purred loudly as Perkins stroked his
thick fur.

"Yes," said the Professor, taking up
the conversation again where it had
been interrupted, "I have always main-
tained that this growing neglect of the

44

classics is one of the worst tendencies
of modern education. Now, take the
study of Homer. What could be more
——? I beg your pardon! Did you
say anything?"

"Oh, no! nothing at all; I quite
agree with you," answered Perkins, confusedly, and he breathed a sigh of relief
as the Professor mounted his hobby
afresh and ambled pleasantly on. For
Perkins had made a discovery.

In stroking the cat his hand had en-
countered what seemed like a hard
lump under the skin of the fore leg.
He felt of it first curiously, then excitedly, then triumphantly. Yes, there
could be no doubt about it, the two
bones of the antebrachium had been
ossified into one, either naturally or as
the result of some accident. There
was a thick ridge running completely

around the limb. Only that morning
Professor Clarkson had lectured on the
fusion of bones, and here was a splendid example of that very thing.

Perkins intended to be a surgeon,
and was devoting himself to biology
with an energy which partially atoned
for the neglect of his other studies.
He felt a wave of professional enthusiasm rise in his heart. What a chance
for original investigation! Such cases
he knew were rare, and he might never
have this opportunity again. Clearly,
Odysseus must be sacrificed on the altar
of science.

His first impulse was to beg the cat
from the Professor. Then he remembered that Mrs. Bancroft was probably
fond of the animal, and might not be
willing to part with him. Perkins reflected. There are, proverbially, three

46

ways of obtaining anything: we may
beg, borrow or steal. Begging was, to
say the least, very uncertain ; borrow-
ing was clearly out of the question.
By the process of elimination Perkins
felt himself forced to adopt the third
method.

But to return a man's hospitality
by stealing his cat! The baseness of
it daunted him. He felt cautiously of
the limb. Yes, the bones were clearly
ossified. "Besides," whispered the
tempter, "you can easily give Mrs.
Bancroft another cat." He cast his
scruples to the winds and began to
consider how the theft might best be
accomplished.

By skillful and apparently innocent
inquiries about the habits of Odysseus,
he learned that the cat was accustomed
to leave the house at night and wander

forth on mysterious nocturnal enter-
prises. In the morning he would
always be found asleep in a particular
corner of the kitchen. How he got in
and out of the house, and what he did
during his wanderings, no one had
been able to discover.

Having learned these facts, Perkins
was not long in resolving on a plan of
action, and about ten o'clock he said
" good night " and departed. As long
as he thought the Professor was watching him he walked steadily in the direction of Morgan Hall. Then, when
he heard the front door close, he returned cautiously and began a careful
patrol of the garden, watching both
the front and rear of the house.

Ten minutes passed — fifteen —
twenty — and still no Odysseus. It
was very cold standing there in the

snow, and he felt his first scruples returning. After all, it was not a very nice thing to steal the cat. It was certainly a poor return for the good dinner he had just eaten. He would go around in the morning and ask the Professor to give him Odysseus, offering in exchange another and more valuable cat. Yes, that was certainly the better plan.

Suddenly he started! Thirty yards away a dark object was slowly moving across the snow. He gave a suppressed whoop and dashed off in pursuit. The snow was very soft and deep so that Odysseus could only flounder slowly along, and in a minute Perkins had him by the neck. But this had not been accomplished without a struggle and considerable noise; and just as he was about to stifle the yowls of the animal in the folds of his ulster, the door of the house opened and the Professor appeared.

"Who's that?" he called out. "What are you doing there?" And then, receiving no answer, he started to investigate.

But Perkins waited not. Holding his hat with one hand, and grasping the loudly protesting Odysseus with the other, he rushed wildly away, and disappeared from the sight of the bewildered Professor behind a clump of trees.

The next morning Perkins was bending over all that remained of the unlucky cat. The fusion of the bones had been perfect, and he eagerly dissected away the muscles in order to get a better view of it. Suddenly the scalpel fell from his hand, and he jumped violently as the mild voice of the Greek Professor said close to his ear — "I was showing Professor Cuttin of Harvard through the laboratory, Mr. Perkins, and I thought perhaps he might be interested in your work."

For the life of him, Perkins could not say a word. He had a wild impulse to throw the cat out of the window, but the Professor had stepped between him and the table. "What are you working on?" he asked, and bent down to examine the animal in the dissecting tray. Alas! there was no mistaking the black and white fur and the little dark spot on the tip of the tail. The Professor rubbed his eyes and looked again. Yes, that was certainly Odysseus.

Some men would have laughed, others would have become angry; the Professor did neither. "I should have told you," he remarked pleasantly to the visitor, "that Mr. Perkins is one of our most zealous students of Biology."

THE SIN OF HOLY HEDGES

The Sin of Holy Hedges.

HEDGES was grinding Greek, as usual, in his room in East. Outspread on the desk before him lay his Sophocles, directly in the range of the big, round spectacles; on one side of the old Grecian his Liddell and Scott, to purchase which he had denied himself the necessities of life (that is, the apparent necessities), and on the other side a translation — closed. In fact, the latter was destined to be opened not more than half a dozen times at the most during the evening, for Hedges was one of those strong-minded young men who are able to keep a trot to use only in cases of absolute need, when the underbrush of idiomatic constructions gets so inextricably tangled as to require Gordian methods. This was Hedges' strong point, self-restraint.

He was probably the only man in East who was grinding at that time. It was one of those soft, mild nights, infrequent enough in the early Berkshire springtime, that, when they come, seem to inspire a sort of complacent laziness quite irresistible. But there was another reason; quite a large number of the fellows had left town for Amherst, to witness a championship game, and those that had remained had scarcely as yet recovered from the epidemic of enthusiasm and cheering which the telegram, just received from the seat of war and bulletined in Watson's, had inaugurated. Occasionally still a straggling " Yums ! Yams ! Yums !" from some irrepressible was borne in to Hedges as he sat at his desk. But the big spectacles remained persistently focused on the Sophocles.

Presently there was a series of kicks on the door, evidently in place of knocks, and a moment later, before Hedges had a chance to respond to them, a youth in a golf suit, with a pipe of sophomorical dimensions in his mouth, entered the room.

"Hello! grubbing?" cried the new-comer, in surprise.

"Yes, won't you sit down, Bald-win?" said Hedges, in his formal way.

Baldwin complied with the spirit, if not with the letter of the request, by flinging himself on the divan and blow-ing smoke rings out of the window into the darkness.

"Say, old man," he began, "we want you to come along later and help us root out the freshmen and make 'em pull up the team. It's a glorious victory, and it'll give 'em a chance to show their college spirit — if they have any, which I doubt." Both fellows were sophomores. "And, by the way, you'll probably be needed to dock that precious room-mate of yours," he added with a laugh. "He went down, didn't he?"

"Yes, he went," answered the other, shortly.

Baldwin looked at his classmate with amusement. He felt tempted to jolly Hedges about exerting his influence on the erring one, but he looked at the firmly closed lips, and thought he had better not. They talked for a few minutes about the game, the prospect for another championship that year, and, after Hedges had renewed his promise to aid in getting out the freshmen, Baldwin left to continue his self-appointed mission among his classmates.

Hedges did not relish Baldwin's remark about his room-mate, though it was not because he thought the prophesy would prove a false one; quite the contrary. But it hurt him to have the matter spoken of in such a flippant way, as if it were of no consequence. Perhaps he imagined a sneer in Baldwin's laugh, which there probably was not. It was a sore point with Hedges, his room-mate's waywardness. He was an older man than Jamieson, and he felt that he ought to have some influence over him. But he had none, that was certain.

He and Jamieson had been friends together at prep. school. There they were much the same sort of fellows;

they had similar pursuits and similar aims; at least there was no such divergence in their manner of life as was noticeable now at the end of sophomore year. But, perhaps, that was due more to the force of external circumstances than to inner tendencies.

Mount Lebanon was of that species of boys' schools which aim not only to give the youth the requisite preparation for admission to college, but also attempt the more difficult task of imparting a moral impetus, calculated to carry him safely through the manifold temptations which may assail him later in his course. Their motto is: "As the twig is bent so will the tree incline;" and the twigs are bent with a vengeance. Result, you have a model set of young men entering college from these institutions — sometimes. Yet, frequently, the result seems to be quite the reverse of the one contemplated. Restraint being removed, some of the young saplings, it is true, remain docilely bent; but others revert to the obstinately vertical position of original sin — and often with remarkable quickness.

Jamieson was one of the latter sort. When he came to college he was like Mr. Seaman's unfortunate poetess; he was in Eve's predicament, and would not be happy till he'd sinned. He was in a mood of revolt. No more of the namby pambyism of Mount Lebanon for him. In short, he felt it was obligatory on him, as a young man who had become his own master, to sow a few wild oats, and he had been sowing assiduously now for nearly two years.

He would tire of it before long, most likely, but while the process continued it was very trying for his conscientious friend.

For Hedges, college was a serious matter, a matter of opportunities and duties. He labored under the delusion that one comes to college primarily to study; an heretical doctrine among undergraduates, though many can always be found who are more or less guilty of putting it into practice — secretly, if not openly. And then there were Y. M. C. A. meetings and class prayer meetings, opportunities not to be neglected. To teach Sunday school in the little school house up on North West Hill was another opportunity, and every Sunday afternoon, rain or shine, found Hedges with Bible and Peloubet under his arm setting out on

his three-mile tramp with the enthusiasm of a missionary in his heart. All
this was easy enough; Hedges took to
it like a duck to water. But some
things he found hard to do. It was
not easy, for instance, to get up and
leave a dormitory room when the rep-
artee got a little coarse, or the anec-
dotes a trifle risqué; and it was harder
still to know that one was called Holy
Hedges in consequence, for Hedges
was quite human under his prematurely
ministerial air. But hardest of all
perhaps, it was to shut his lips tightly
together and say nothing when he saw
his friend doing things he should not.
But Hedges did all these and other hard
things, because he considered it his
duty to do them — and Hedges always
did his duty at any cost.

Towards half-past ten a crowd of

sophomores came through East, making as much noise as possible, and incidentally assuring themselves that all
the freshmen were out and ready to
pull up the team. They rushed up the
stairs shouting "All out!" a great many
times, and making considerable needless racket with their feet. On the top
floor some one found two ash cans that
had been left out of the rooms inad-
vertently, and down stairs they were
sent, making the noise of a dozen boiler
shops on the iron sheathing of the
steps. On the floor below, some one
else, whose brains had just escaped
being knocked out by the cans in their
mad career, picked them up and sent
them down another flight. This was
celebrating the glorious victory.

Some one began kicking mightily at
the door of the room next to that of

Hedges. "Get to hell out, you sleepy freshman," he shouted. Potter, blasé youth that he was, had gone to bed some time since, remarking that he'd a hang sight rather be sleeping at midnight than pulling those lazy beggars up Consumption Hill. But the invitation of the enthusiastic committee was urgent, punctuated as it was with vigorous kicks that tested the strength of his oak, and was not to be slighted. At first Potter pretended to be asleep, but at last when the lock seemed about ready to break at any moment, a stone came cleanly through his window and landed in his wash bowl, deciding him that it was necessary to capitulate. "All right," he grunted, "just let me get my clothes on, can't you?" And he began tumbling into his trousers, boots and sweater.

Baldwin opened Hedges' door. "Come on," he shouted, and slammed the door again.

Hedges waited five minutes to finish the work he was engaged upon, and then got up from his desk and began to put up his books and get ready to go out to join the crowd who were now well on their way toward the station. He had just completed an orderly arrangement of the things on his desk when he heard a light tap on his door.

"Come in," he shouted somewhat crossly. This going down to meet the team was a rather foolish business anyway. A moment later the door was opened and an elderly man entered, followed by a slender girl of sixteen or seventeen.

"I beg your pardon for not coming to the door," said Hedges, somewhat abashed. " I. thought it was one of the fellows."

" So it is," answered the elderly gentleman, " One of the old fellows — And you, I presume, are Mr. Hedges."

Hedges replied in the affirmative.

"And you are wondering, I see, who it is that is calling on you at such an unseasonable hour," he continued, noticing the perplexed look on Hedges' face. " I am Harry Jamieson's father, and this my daughter, Dorothy."

Hedges shook hands with both of them, and begged them to be seated.

" Harry is not in now," he explained, " in fact is out of town. He went to Amherst this morning with the rest to see the game, and has not got back yet. I suppose he will return with the others on the midnight train."

" Ah, to be sure. I had quite forgotten that there was a ball game at Amherst to-day. Harry wrote that he was intending to go down this year." Mr. Jamieson took out his watch. "After eleven," he exclaimed, " I really did not think it was quite so late as that. We owe you an apology, I am sure, for intruding at such an hour, but having gone so far I am going to venture a bit farther, and ask you if we may remain here till my son arrives ? "

"Yes, certainly," answered Hedges. If there was any lack of cordiality in the reply, Mr. Jamieson, evidently, did notice it.

He went on to explain the reason for his visit. He had been asked to exchange pulpits for the following day with the pastor of a church in North Adams, and so had taken the occasion to pay a visit to Williamstown at the same time, and to bring his daughter with him, as he had long promised her. He had written when the arrangements had been completed, but evidently the letter had not come when Harry left town. They had come over from North Adams a short time before, and were staying for the night at Prof. Harvey's, an old friend since the time of college days. Late as it was, Dorothy had insisted that they should walk over to the dormitory, on the possible chance that Harry might still be up. They had seen the light at the window and inferred that he was.

Hedges appeared to be listening to Mr. Jamieson, but in reality he was paying little attention. He was thinking of Baldwin's disagreeable remark

about his room-mate's probable condition on his return to town, and, what
was more, he was forced to admit that
his own apprehensions pointed in the
same direction. The victory, a close
one and rather unexpected, the crowd
of fellows he had gone with, everything
forced the conclusion ; experience had
taught him temptations considerably
less strong than those that lay in the
present circumstances would have been
sufficient to insure it. But what could
he do? To tell the truth, it did not
occur to him that there was anything
he could do. Artifice of any sort was
a thing so far removed from Hedges'
character that the possibility even of
practicing any deception on the elder
Jamieson did not enter his mind. If
Harry came home drunk on the night
his father and sister chose to visit him

there was nothing he could do about it. Still, when he pictured to himself the scene, from the secular, so to speak, and as yet little explored region of his conscience, a voice cried to him that it was wrong to passively allow the catastrophe to come; it would be nothing short of cruelty toward the father, worse than cruelty toward this sensitive girl, and rank infidelity besides toward his friend. But the messenger did not have the usual credentials — and then what could he do anyway?

They talked the usual commonplaces; about the beauty of the Berkshire country in springtime; the change time had made in the college and town; prospective improvements and the rest. Mr. Jamieson bore the weight of the conversation; Hedges felt in no mood for talking, and Dorothy, who had evidently been brought up in the good old-fashioned rule, "children should be seen and not heard," gave herself up to silent but absorbing observation of the contents of the room. Hedges unconsciously tried to keep the conversation impersonal, but it was in vain. It was Harry, Mr. Jamieson was thinking of, and of him he was determined to speak.

They had been talking of the many delightful walks the country afforded.

"The value to a young man," Mr. Jamieson was saying, "which a four years' residence in a college like Williams has, lies of course, first of all in the opportunities for study and intellectual advancement which it offers. First of all, I repeat, for I have no patience with the men who neglect such opportunities. Yet there are other things, possibly of nearly as great value in the end, subtle influences which pervade the place, giving it its character, and which cannot help affecting those who live here for four years. One of the best of these, it seems to me, is the influence of nature. I wonder how many men it has inspired. If Bryant did not write Thanatopsis while sitting in Flora's Glen, and I believe the higher criticism would have us doubt the story, at least he may have been inspired to do it by a visit there — at any rate I like to think so. But there is a higher sort of inspiration than that which results in the expression of the best thoughts in poetry, and that is the inspiration which leads to the formation of high ideals which express themselves in right living. You see, I cannot help preaching," he added, smiling. "But I speak from my own experience. It was on a trip up Greylock, just when we entered the Hopper — I remember the time very well — it was a glorious autumn day, with the foliage as you know it — that I finally decided to make my life work the preaching of the Gospel."

"We hope Harry will choose the ministry," said Dorothy. It was the first time the girl had spoken, and the words were uttered almost unconsciously. A few moments before, she had risen and become absorbed in looking at a cluster of photographs over Harry's desk. Hedges watched her as she took down the two or three pictures of her brother's girl friends whom she evidently did not know, and studied them with tender, half jealous curiosity.

The corporate interest which her "we" implied struck him keenly.

For a moment he had a notion of telling Mr. Jamieson, so that he might take the girl away, but the thought of betraying his friend, and needlessly, perhaps, made him hesitate. He was afraid of the result. Occasionally gleams of hardness and rigorousness had shown themselves in the father's conversation, evincing an unrelenting nature under his apparent gentleness of manner. Harry was thoughtless, but not a bad fellow at heart, and an over-severe punishment, injudiciously timed, might do no end of injury. No, he would risk it. Harry might come home all right. He thought he had seen in him a growing weariness for the sort of fun he had been amusing himself with — Hedges was a born

75

physician of souls, and watched his friend for symptoms continually. But the hope had little consolation in it. At heart he did not believe it.

"I suppose we old fellows," Mr. Jamieson was prosing away, "are inclined to view the past through rose-colored spectacles, but I, for one, cannot help thinking that there is not the strong religious spirit pervading the college life that there used to be. In my day there was much opposition to religion from some quarters, but not that spirit of indifference which seems so rife at present. An indifference in matters of creed, if you like, which is sure to react on morals. And indifference is more dangerous, don't you think so, than the best directed opposition that is open and tangible."

"Yes, I've always thought so."

76

Hedges had made the same criticism a dozen times, but somehow he resented it now. It seemed a narrow one.

The older man appeared to appreciate the unuttered qualification. " I may do you injustice," he explained. "Young men are not so enthusiastic about anything as they were in times gone past, or at least do not express their enthusiasm so freely. But, perhaps, the feeling is just as strong as ever. I hope so. Now, Harry scarcely ever talks to me of his own accord on religious subjects. Yet he is a good boy, and I would not like to believe that he does not think about such things."

Hedges said nothing, and Mr. Jamieson asked : " You are intending entering the ministry, are you not ? "

"I hope to be able to," Hedges answered.

"I am glad to hear it. I understood you were, and I assure you I feel that it is very fortunate that my son should constantly associate with one who has a definite, serious purpose in view. Harry is only a boy, scarcely formed in character yet, and he needs the influence of an older, steadier man."

Hedges got up abruptly and went to the window. "They should be here in a few minutes," he said. Under the circumstances, he could hardly be expected to relish the compliment. But there was a keener sting in the remark than one would perhaps imagine. It forced the old question which he had asked himself so many times. "If I have no influence over this boy whom I know so well, how can I expect to prevail over strong men with evil habits, deep-rooted in their natures?" And he had no such influence, not a particle. But yet how could one hope to gain effectiveness if not by a consecration of one's self to the cause of religion? Was not that the road that had always been pointed out to him as the only possible one? He believed it was, himself, but sometimes there came doubts.

The Gym. clock had struck twelve some minutes before, and already the noise of fireworks and cheering could be heard faintly down toward the railroad station. Mr. Jamieson and Dorothy came and stood beside Hedges at the window.

"There is to be a demonstration on account of the victory," Hedges explained. "Almost every one who remained in town has gone down to the station. The horses will be unharnessed from the barge that brings up the team, and some of the fellows will pull it up to the gymnasium, while the rest march along beside and make as much racket as possible. They will be in sight in a moment."

"Harry will be with the rest?" Dorothy asked.

Hedges looked at her expectant face. "Yes, I suppose so," he answered, and turned away quickly.

By leaning out of the window they could get a good view of the procession, if it could be so called, as it advanced up Main street. The central figure was the barge containing the nine heroes of the day and the substitutes, who would have been heroes if they had been given a chance. In front of the barge was a long line of freshmen pulling at the rope which was fastened to the tongue of the wagon. On all sides, behind, before, in the street and on the sidewalks, were crowds of fellows blowing tin horns, exploding fireworks promiscuously in all directions without regard for consequences, and dancing like dervishes. The air was thick with dust and gunpowder smoke, and ruddy with colored fire; the remarkable feat of the " Grand old Duke of York, who had ten thousand men," was celebrated in song over and over again, enthusiastically, if not harmoniously. The barge, with its escort, was now half-way up Consumption Hill. Here was the tug. But in a moment it had reached the top and then began rushing down the incline toward the Gym.

Before long the noise of feet was heard on the stairways, and doors began to be opened and slammed. Hedges listened.

"Damn it, I'm not going to bed. I'm goin' out'n' have a hell of a time," some one cried, in a high-keyed, childish voice. It was little freshman Hawkins. The rest of the party laughed boisterously. Another began to sing "Some vaunt the crimson, some the blue," but missed a step and came to a short stop. Hedges recognized the singer as Ned Allerton, and he knew that Jamieson would be with him. The crowd was worse than usual to-night.

They came on stumbling up the stairs. Hedges got up. He didn't know just what he would do, but at any rate he was going to keep Harry Jamieson from coming into the room.

" I — I hope you'll excuse me a moment," he stammered, " I want to speak to one of the fellows before he goes to his room." He felt that he was blushing, and that Mr. Jamieson was wondering what rattled him so. In a moment he had slipped out of the room.

When he saw his friend, Hedges decided what to do. A few moments later he came back to his room with his courage screwed up and a lie ready to tell. It was a big one, and not so very plausible, and it might not deceive the father, but it would, at least, make him take the girl away and prevent a scene.

" I am sorry to tell you," he said, looking Mr. Jamieson squarely in the face, " that Harry did not come back to-night with the rest." He hesitated, and then continued, trying to assume his natural tone: "I went out to speak to one of the fellows and chanced to meet Griswold, who was just coming here with a message from Harry, that he had decided to stay with a friend in Amherst over Sunday. Of course, he did not know you were coming," he added weakly, seeing the look of disappointment in Dorothy's face.

"It is very unfortunate that he should have chosen this particular Sunday. I suppose it means that we shan't see him this time, Dolly."

Hedges studied the man's face. He could not decide whether or no the deception had succeeded. They left in a moment, and Hedges went out and found Jamieson and got him to bed.

The next morning Hedges was spending the time between breakfast and the hour for chapel service in writ-

ing his usual weekly letter home. It
was after half-past nine and his room-
mate's bedroom door was still closed.
Presently he heard a tap which he
recognized. He got up this time and
went to the door himself instead of
calling "Come in," as usual. It was
Mr. Jamieson, as he had expected—
but alone.

"Come in, won't you?" asked
Hedges. He did not say, "I am glad
to see you"—he was not going to tell
lies gratuitously at any rate.

Mr. Jamieson came in and sat down;
neither said a word for a moment, but
Hedges knew what was coming.

At last Mr. Jamieson spoke. "I
have come to talk with you, Mr.
Hedges, very seriously. I shall be
quite frank with you, and I trust you
will be equally so with me." He

paused a moment. "I could scarcely help knowing that there were several men who came into the dormitory last night under the influence of drink. I was not mistaken in that, was I?"

"No, there were a few, I am sorry to say."

"You said that my son had sent you word that he was intending to stay out of town over Sunday. You will pardon me for harboring such a suspicion if it is a wrong one, but I have not been able to rid myself of the thought that you were concealing something from me. I am probably mistaken. And in that case I can only beg your forgiveness, yet I could not refrain from coming to you and asking you to assure me of it. Needless to say, I shall accept your word implicitly and

86

without questioning of any sort." Mr. Jamieson waited for a reply.

Hedges looked him squarely in the face, as on the night before. "It was quite true what I said," he answered, "your son stayed at Amherst last night — at least such was his message to me." There was a touch of contempt in his voice. What right had this man to try to force him into a betrayal of his friend?

But his conscience troubled him just a little when the other got up, and, extending his hand, said, in his former cordial voice, "I am glad to hear it, Mr. Hedges. More glad than you can well imagine. It has relieved my mind wonderfully. I cannot tell you how much." And he took a hurried leave, explaining that a man was waiting be- low to drive him over to North Adams.

Hedges sat down to his writing. In a few minutes Jamieson come out into the study half dressed. He stood in the middle of the room with his hand on the table, looking down at the floor. Hedges continued his letter. "Your father has just been here," he said, in a matter of fact way, without looking up.

"Yes, I recognized the governor's voice," Jamieson replied. Neither spoke for a moment.

"Phil, old man, you're a brick," Jamieson burst out impetuously.

Hedges kept on with his writing, and made no reply, but there was something in the voice and the attitude of the boy that pleased him mightily. It gave him a sense of effectiveness that was new to him; conscience or no conscience, he had learned something, and a something, by the way, quite necessary for him to learn sooner or later. Hedges had a dim sort of realization of this fact, and it gave him genuine satisfaction — for, after all, to learn was the purpose for which Hedges came to college.

CONCERNING A FRESHMAN

Concerning a Freshman.

"FRESHMEN," remarked Campbell from the divan, "are necessary evils. Necessary, because the college must be perpetuated; evils, because — well, because they are freshmen."

"So, that's what has kept you quiet for the last fifteen minutes," said Thompson; "really, Campbell, if I couldn't make a better epigram than that after a quarter of an hour's meditation I'd give up trying to."

"What's the matter now?" chimed in Perkins. "Has one of them been fresh to you? Take my advice and wear corduroy trousers. Of course, no one will take you for a senior even then, but they can't help seeing that you're an upper classman."

"You go to thunder!" said Campbell good naturedly. "Give me some tobacco and I'll tell you the particular application of my general remark. Do any of you know Witherbee?" he asked, as he lit his pipe and leaned back among the cushions.

"Yes," answered Green, "he has the next room, and I've seen him in the hall once or twice; what about him?"

"Why, he's one of those fellows," replied Campbell, "who come to this place with their ideas of Williams formed from a perusal of the cata- logue that the registrar sends to the principal of their high school. I don't believe he ever heard of college customs, or, at any rate, he hasn't the least idea of observing them. In fact, he publicly informed several persons that he considered himself quite as good as a senior."

"It seems to me," said Green, "that a course in common sense would be a splendid addition to the curriculum of the average prep. school. Some of the freshmen that we get here appear to be utterly lacking in it. Now, I presume that our friend Witherbee believes that he is acting quite an heroic part in taking the stand he does."

"I'm sure of it," said Thompson; "in fact he told me himself that he considered it unmanly to allow any one to interfere with his personal rights. I'm proud to add that I never cracked a smile. What has he been doing anyway?" he added.

"Why, the first thing he did," answered Campbell, "was to tack up his card outside his door, and it was promptly torn down. Then he appeared on Weston Field in corduroy trousers, and disappeared without them ; after that, to cap the climax, he smoked a pipe in the street, and the sophomores took it away from him, whereupon my young friend called them several unpleasant names, and informed them that he intended to do as he pleased."

" He certainly is fresh," said Thompson, "but he's not a bad sort of a fellow. Some one at home gave him a letter to me, and, of course, I did what I could in helping him furnish his room and find a boarding place. The trouble is that he has come here without the slightest idea of what college life is like."

"Well," said Green, "he'll have a lively time finding out. I heard the sophs were going to visit him this evening."

"He must have been reading some of those fool stories about the evils of hazing," said Perkins. "You know the style: 'The Boy Who Would Not Be Hazed,' with illustrations showing the heroic freshman hurling defiance (and other things) at a crowd of brutal sophomores, three of whom he has knocked down. Why do people write such stuff anyway?"

"I'm sure I don't know," answered Green, "and what is more I don't care very much, either. I was invited here to eat a rabbit, and I'm not going to be sidetracked into a discussion on freshmen. You cut up the cheese and I'll get out the rest of the eatables."

Concerning a Freshman.

In a short time Thompson, who excelled in such matters, was bending over the chafing-dish, while the others assisted him with advice as to the seasoning.

"Now, then, Perkins," called out the cook, "hurry up with that beer! Not so much! This isn't soup we're making! Get the mustard, quick, some one; it's in that brown paper on the table. A little more pepper, Green. More yet! Great Heavens, man! don't put in the whole two ounces. Now wait a minute, it's nearly done. Ready with your plates! There you are! You'd better eat it before it cools."

The man who makes a Welsh rabbit has no time to think of anything else; and the same is true, in a lesser degree, of the man who eats one. It was not until the five plates were deposited clean upon the table that the subject of Witherbee was brought up again.

"I feel sorry for that freshman," said Campbell, in the tone of fatherly patronage that upper classmen learn to employ when speaking of those two or three years behind them; "I shouldn't think his first term would give him any very deep love for Williams."

"It won't," answered Bronson; "he probably thinks this is the worst hole he ever got into. But if he has good stuff in him he'll come out of it all right in the end."

"That's just it," said Thompson. "If he has good stuff in him. But supposing he hasn't? I wonder if many men get so sick of the mill they're put through freshman year that they clear out in disgust."

Concerning a Freshman.

"Lots of them," said Campbell; "but they are the ones who ought never to have been allowed to come to college at all. This isn't a hot-house, you know. We're not sup-posed to be a nursery for freaks. The college takes a hundred, more or less, crude and unformed boys, and turns them out in four years with their ef-fectiveness doubled and trebled, and a sort of general superficial polish that people call college training. That's all it tries to do, and if the weak ones break during the process you can't blame the system.

"It makes me tired to see the way people bring up a boy, without any idea of what the world is like, and then look surprised and grieved when he goes to the devil the minute he leaves home. While I'm just as fond of Williams as any of you, and think there's no place like it, I don't imagine for a moment that it's going to work miracles. You can't expect this college to take the place of a nurse, and as for its trying to be father and mother and condensed milk to all the fools that come here, it's simply ridiculous!"

"Now, fellows!" cried Bronson, "a Williams cheer with Campbell on the end."

"That was a burst," admitted Campbell, joining in the laugh; "but I get hot sometimes when people talk rot about the evils of college life. As for hazing, I've never heard of any one being hurt by it since I've been here, and there is nothing like it in the world to correct swelled head. A man may come here conceited, and leave here conceited, but at least he has an intervening period of sanity."

"When you get through settling the affairs of the nation, Campbell," said Perkins, "I wish you would come to the window and see the fun. There's a crowd of sophs in front of the Gym., and I imagine they're getting ready to visit our friend in the next room."

The four looked out of the window. It was too dark to distinguish faces, but they could make out a group of men gathered on the gymnasium steps giving their class yell.

Newcomers constantly arrived, and when forty or fifty were assembled, they started for "Hell's Entry" of Morgan Hall, and came pouring up the narrow stairs, while a general bolting of freshman doors, and extinguishing of freshman lights heralded their approach. 102

"Now he's in for it," said Green, "Lord, what a noise they're making!"

Up the stairs rushed the sophomores shouting and singing. "Witherbee! Witherbee! we want Witherbee!" they yelled; then they stopped before his room. "Open up there!" they called, pounding and kicking on the door.

No answer.

"Come! Come! Open the door or we'll break it in!" they shouted.

Still no answer.

"Now, fellows!" said some one, "all together! One! Two! Three!"

Twenty men flung themselves against the door. It held for a moment, then burst open, and the crowd rushed in.

"Look here," said Thompson, "let's go in and see that they don't go too far."

"Don't you do it," answered Perkins; "they won't hurt him, and if ever a man needed a calling down he does."

However, they went out into the hall where they could hear all that went on.

"I tell you I won't," said Witherbee passionately. "Bullies! Cowards! Leave my room!"

A chorus of derisive yells, followed by a half a dozen orders flung at him at once was the only answer.

"No," he cried again, "I won't sing songs! I won't make a speech! I'm not going to be bullied by any one! Get out I tell you!"

The yell which followed was not quite so good natured as the first; the crowd was getting angry.

"Look here," said some one, "we've

fooled with this man long enough. If he won't be decent he's got to take the consequences. Now, then, fresh, will you sing or speak? Hurry up, we can't wait all night!"

"No!" answered Witherbee, "I won't do anything! You're a pack of ———." The rest of the sentence was lost in the sound of a struggle.

"O, damn it all!" said Thompson, "they'll hurt him! I'm going in."

He pushed through the men outside the door and elbowed his way to the center of the group around Witherbee. Then some one in the crowd recognized him, and the noise stopped.

"See here, fellows!" he said, "You've gone far enough; you don't want to hurt him."

"O nonsense, Thompson," answered a man from the crowd; "it'll do him good. He's the freshest man in college." "That's so!" came from a dozen men. "If we stop now he'll be worse than ever."

"You've gone far enough," repeated Thompson. "You're not going to do anything more to him to-night. Get out!"

They didn't like it; but he was a senior, and, after a moment of hesitation, they departed, to console themselves with the freshmen in the next entry. Witherbee picked himself up.

" O, thank you, Mr. Thompson!" he exclaimed excitedly. " Thank you for rescuing me from those bullies! If ever I can do anything for you just let me ——." He stopped abruptly, for Thompson was not paying the slightest attention to his thanks, nor to the hand he had half extended.

Concerning a Freshman.

" Witherbee," he said, " I think you are, without exception, the blamedest fool I have seen since I entered college!" And he followed the sophomores out of the room.

THE VALLEY OF DECISION

The Valley of Decision.

WHEN Paul Lorrimer received Mrs. Endicott's invitation to come up and stay at her country house in Williamstown for a week or so, about commencement time, he decided, without much hesitation, to accept. He had not been back to the quiet little town in the five years that he had been an alumnus, and he had a great desire to see the old place again. In addition to this loyal sentiment Mrs. Endicott always made a charming hostess, and there were to be other pleasant people, he heard, staying at her house at the same time.

But he did not happen to know that

Miss Sterling was to be among the number. That was a surprise await-ing him on his arrival. It was a bit prophetic, if they both had only known it, that she should have been the first person he saw when the trap that had brought him up from the sta-tion pulled up under the porte-cochére of The Hillocks. "Why, Pollie," he said, as he took her hand, "I didn't know that I was to see *you* here.'

"It's as much of a surprise to me as to any one," Miss Sterling answered. "Elsie Winthrop was taken ill at the last minute, and Aunt Geraldine tele-graphed me to come and take her place. It wasn't entirely flattering, was it? But," she added with a sud-den upward look, "I wanted to come." The astute Lorrimer understood the look.

"Pollie Sterling is an awfully at-
tractive little girl," he said to himself
later, as he was dressing for dinner.
"But I hope she clearly understands
that all that nonsense we indulged in
down at St. Augustine last winter was
— nonsense. You never can quite
trust these girls, though, who are just
young enough to take life seriously.
I hope the fascinations of some chap
in a black gown and mortar board
will relieve me from all necessity of
enlightening her. But if it is necessary —" He broke off his soliloquy
abruptly. A man tying an evening
cravat before a looking-glass cannot be
impressive, even to himself.

That night, after dinner, when the
others had gone out onto the piazza,
Miss Sterling went to the piano and
sang Charminade's song about the girl

who broke her heart waiting for a
lover who never came, and Lorrimer
decided, between whiffs of smoke,
that, after all, he had not come to
Williamstown to impose a disagreeable duty upon himself. It is sur-
prising with what promptness the
members of a house party understand
each other. After a day or two certain combinations are received in a
matter-of-fact, unquestioning way, and
it is perfectly understood that no one
will poach on the preserves of another's
monopoly. The advantages of this
system are, of course, relative to the
character of one's " corner," and occasionally — but that is exactly why one
should exercise discretion in accepting
invitations to country houses.

Pending the arrival of the seniorial
middleman, who should divert Miss

Sterling's emotional attention, Lorrimer had let matters drift back into their old course. It was made so easy that it was almost unconscious. And why should he spoil a simple, pleasant friendship with some bungling prudishness? Lorrimer was well on in the middle age of his youth, yet he used the word with a half sincerity. It was not because he did not understand, either, but rather because it had never occurred to him to apply the excellent epigrams he had made concerning life to himself.

Most experience is divided into a before and an after by a climax.

And Lorrimer's climax came.

The fellows at his fraternity house had arranged a dance and most of the people staying at The Hillocks decided to go. "Of course you and Pollie will go," Mrs. Endicott had said to Lorrimer when they were all talking it over. The "of course" had stung a little. He would have preferred if everything had not been entirely taken for granted. Pollie's attitude annoyed him too. He kept away from the house that day and, when they met at dinner, he confined the conversation strictly within the bounds of impersonalities. The next day he spent playing golf with Jack Ellis. The one little glimpse he had of Pollie made him miserably remorseful, but he felt that he was taking the right course. That night when he came up to his room to dress for the dance, he found lying among the silver things on his dressing table some white sweet flowers. He knew that she had sent them for his buttonhole, but he put them in a glass of water instead.

Lorrimer drove over from The Hillocks to the dance with Mrs. Endicott and her niece. Pollie had hardly spoken to him all the evening, but now she was unusually gay, and rattled on about everything and nothing, with reckless inconsequence. "Pollie," Mrs. Endicott said, "you are as excited as if you were going to your first dance. Ah, here we are! Tell him when we shall want the carriage, Paul, please."

The pretty house was bright with lights and gay with laughter when they came in. In the long room, where they were dancing, they had filled the big fireplace with flowers, and the walls were nearly hidden with college banners and festoons of evergreen.

Lorrimer danced first with Pollie and then gave her up to the others. He did not see her again until he went later to claim a promised dance. "I am tired," she said, "I would much rather go outside and rest. Do you mind not dancing it?"

There was a little group of close-set trees on the lawn near the house, and some one had put seats under them. Out of the leafy dimness of their boughs some colored lanterns glowed like great globe-like fruit.

"Let's go over there," Pollie said, when they had gotten out on to the piazza.

The music came to them faintly, out there under the trees. The warm darkness seemed to have grown sensuously tender with it. From where they were sitting they could see the yellow lights of the house blaze out into the night, and sometimes, over the wail of the violins, came the crowded sound of the chatter of many voices. Pollie had taken off her long gloves and had lain them limply across her knees. She bent forward, smoothing the wrinkles out of them with a kind of nervous indifference. The light of one of the lanterns, hung in the leaves above her, fell on her soft hair, and caressed the smooth, babyish roundness of her throat and breast. Lorrimer, leaning back in the shadow, regarded her with a sort of pitying admiration.

"Would you mind if I lit a cigarette?" he inquired. He did not care about smoking, but he felt the conversational blank must be filled somehow.

The girl turned to him quickly. "Why are you so formal? Have I ever cared? Have I ever stopped you doing anything you wanted?"

Lorrimer smiled. It was his theory that a man should always indulge women as long as it did not give him too much trouble. There was a moment's silence. The sob of the waltz music thrilled the night and made it pulsate with answering rapture. "Youth! Youth!" the violins seemed to be sighing. "So soon lost! So soon lost! Love and youth! Love and youth!" The music caught at the girl's heart convulsively. She crushed the soft gloves between her hands. "It is always this way," she said with hurried vehemence. "I do all the caring and you —"

"Is this apropos of cigarettes, or of nothing?" Lorrimer asked quickly. He wanted to avert the melodrama if possible. She did not hear him.

"Look," she went on. "You are

older than I. You know more of the world and people. Perhaps I am not like all the others. Maybe I have amused you. Perhaps you have never realized it, but you have made me love you. Do you understand, *love you?* I know I haven't any decency or I wouldn't tell this to you. I don't care for decency or anything else. I love you!" Her voice shrilled softly with the defiance of desperation.

Lorrimer threw his half-smoked cigarette away. He was enough of a man to be more sorry than flattered by what he had heard. He would have given much to have known the right thing to say; a sick feeling of shame came over him and a wordless tenderness. The other had covered her face and was crying, softly and brokenly.

Lorrimer drew away one of the little cold hands, still wet with her tears.

"Don't cry," he said with gentle firmness. "You really mustn't, you know. How are we to go back and face all those people if you do? There! Now we can talk it all over quietly and perhaps we can understand each other better. You say you love me. Can you tell me why — at first, I mean?"

She had straightened up and had stopped crying, although her lips were still working tremulously. There were white roses pinned to her gown and taking one, she began to tear it to pieces, petal by petal. After a little pause she answered him.

"It sounds silly, but it was your dancing at first, and then — then other things. And then I knew that you were my ideal." Lorrimer could have laughed there in the shadow, but the pathos of the little fluttering hands deterred him.

"And I am that now, and you want to marry me?" He asked the question quite simply. He thought it better if they left nothing unsaid.

Pollie looked up and met his eyes bravely. "Yes," she said. "You are the best and finest and —"

"Wait!" Lorrimer said. "Wait! You don't know me yet." He had decided that she should know. "I suppose that if I were to tell you that I'm none of these good things, you wouldn't believe me."

The girl shook her head, smiling faintly. "No," she said. "I won't—"

"Of course not. We never believe anything evil about our ideals, until

we have ceased to have them. Never-
theless, it's not true — I'm very far
from being even respectably virtuous,
and certainly I'm not fine in any way.
There is really no reason why you
should make anything more of me
than of the twenty-odd other men who
have asked you to dance, and have
sent you flowers occasionally."

"Ah! But I know you too well to
believe you, now. You aren't like any
of those others — not like any one else
in the whole world. How can you be?
I don't love any of them, and I do
love you." Her eyes were shining
like stars, and leaning forward, she
rested her hand on his knee. Lorrimer saw that another method of procedure was necessary.

"My dear," he said, "will you allow
me to talk to you just as your father

might? I'm old enough to be at least your older brother."

"Yes," assented Pollie, quietly. "Go on."

"Do you know you don't really love this — er — person we have been talking about? He isn't your 'ideal' at all. He merely happened to step into your life when you were in need of a figure to wear the costume your imagination had made, and masquerade as your ideal. Very soon you would have seen for yourself how badly the costume fitted — and then you would have blamed him for being an impostor. It's not me you're loving, dear, but your idea of me, and if I let you go on thinking as you do, it would merely hurt us both."

"Why do you talk to me in this way?" she broke out, passionately.

"Because you are a sweet, simple little girl, and I care for you too much to let you think you love me, and that your heart is broken because I can't feel for you in the same way."

"If it is not love — what is it, then?" she asked, almost harshly.

"Just a part of your youth, little one," he answered, gravely. "Just a part of the moonlight, and roses, and white frocks, and waltz music. A very sweet and beautiful part, and something you'll remember some day very tenderly — but no more love than those lights in there where they're dancing are the sun. Can you believe me?" His tone had become very earnest.

"Yes," she answered, listlessly, "I believe you — anything, always."

They sat silent again until she had

pulled the last petal from the rose in her hand; then she asked, very quietly and slowly: "Do you think I'll ever know this other — love — now?"

Lorrimer took her hand into his. "I can ask no greater happiness for my dear friend than that, some time, she may," he said.

Withers came through the trees behind them just then. "Oh, here you are!" he said. "They're just going to begin our dance, and I've been looking for you everywhere."

Pollie stood up, sweeping the white rose petals from her lap as she did so. "I'm all ready," she said. "I'm sorry you had such a bother to find me. Mr. Lorrimer has just been teaching me a new game. Good bye, Mr. Lorrimer," she said to him, "thank you so much for the lesson. I'm afraid I was very stupid at first, but — I — I — understand perfectly now," and she laughed.

When they had gone, Lorrimer settled back in his old seat again. "I'm glad she laughed," he said, half aloud. "When a woman laughs, because she is afraid she will cry if she doesn't, she has learned how to take care of herself." His eye fell on the flowerless rose-stem on the seat beside him. He took it into his hand for a moment.

"Poor little rose," he said, softly. "I am sorry it had to be pulled to pieces; it was so pretty — too pretty to last," he added, under his breath.

THE CONQUEST

129

The Conquest.

THERE comes in the lives of most of us, after we have nibbled all the frosting off the cake, and before we have gotten to like plain bread and butter, a time that is, perhaps, the most trying we will ever experience. We are then in a sort of emotional hobble-de-hoy period, for which there is little help or sympathy to be gained from the outside world. If one happens to be in college, when he goes through this unpleasant adjusting of himself to his intellectual environment, he is lucky, for there are so many doing the same thing that he is hardly noticed. It seems to be the chief use of college, anyway, to supply a safe place for one to recover from one's extreme youth.

But all this is in Joe Thayer's story. It was one of those gray, inhospitable days in late autumn, while he was in the Gym. dressing after a discouraging practice game, that Thayer came to the conclusion that life — college life — was not worth the living. That is a somewhat uninspiring outlook to take, especially when one has advanced no further towards the end than the first term of his junior year. Thayer was not cheered with the prospect. He hurried his dressing to escape from the crowded room, heavy with the odor of liniments and littered with dirty foot ball clothes.

It was dreary enough outside, with little bleak whirls of dust and dead

leaves along the walks, and the wind
muttering in the bare trees. The
lights were already showing in Hopkins as Thayer went across to Morgan, although it was yet comparatively
early.

He hoped he would find his room
empty; he wanted to be quiet before
he faced the hubbub at the training
table later. But he was disappointed.
Bradford Gray and Ned Vernon were
there, both, apparently, perfectly at
home. "We have been waiting for
that wandering room-mate of yours
nearly an hour," Vernon said from the
window; "he promised to be here at
four."

"That's why we oughtn't to have
expected him," Gray broke in, in the
finitive, assured manner of a man who
gave the last word. "Only the unex-

pected occurs." Vernon laughed. He took a cigarette from his case and lit it. He always smoked cigarettes with a pungent, heavy smoke. Gray had called the odor the very essence of Bohemianism once.

"Bradford," Vernon said, "you're too clever to be allowed to go about unmuzzled; you're an humiliation as a conversational example."

"Conversation ought to be like a Chéret poster — blocked in in broad quick color with little regard for the details," answered Gray.

He was a small, dark man with a drawling, insistent voice that was impossible to escape. He had a knack of saying half truths in a terse, convincing way that passed for cleverness. He wrote occasionally for little mushroom magazines with gaudy covers and

limited circulation, and his pose was
that of a literary cynic. The most
charitable of the men who knew him
said that there really wasn't any harm
in him, but the others disliked him
with a heartiness that would have been
franker had they not been secretly
afraid of him. Unpopularity, however, did not disturb Gray's self-respect in the least. He managed to turn
it into a tribute paid by mediocrity to
a dominant personality.

Ned Vernon and he were insepa-
rable. They were sufficiently alike
to thoroughly appreciate each other,
and Vernon was just weak enough not
to rebel against Gray's leadership.
Lately Stafford, Thayer's room-mate,
had been taken into their partnership.
They had a commonality of taste for
refined things to start with, and Gray

managed the rest so successfully that
the result had been brought about almost unconsciously. It fell out that
Stafford's and Thayer's room had become a sort of rallying place, and the
three were together constantly. Thayer
they accepted as a necessary evil.

It was always difficult for Joe Thayer
to observe the ordinary decencies of
hospitality toward these friends of
Stafford's. There was nothing subtle about Thayer,— his mind was as
straightforward as his face, and his
intellect refused to play practical
jokes upon itself. He thought as
simply as he spoke. When Bradford
Gray had said that his mind was as
uncompromising as a right-angled tri-
angle, he had come nearer the truth
than was his wont.

His sentiments in regard to his

room-mate's new friends were definite
enough, certainly. It filled him with
an unreasoning anger when he thought
of them. The number of men Thayer
admired and liked was large,— but the
number of his friends was small. He
had taken Stafford into his affection
with an entireness that almost was
pathetic.

To-day, especially, he was least prepared to be even ordinarily civil to
them. He sat staring out into the
gathering darkness, hardly speaking.
" Mark how the noble brow is dark
with sadness," Vernon said to Gray.
"Can it be that he has not come off
victor in the arena this afternoon ? "

" Impossible that the mere fortunes
of war should ruffle his classic calm,"
Gray answered. The clock was ringing out the hour. Gray pulled him-

self slowly up from the depths of
the Morris chair he was occupying.
"Duty calls me and I must go," he
said. "What a lot of valuable time
one wastes doing one's duty, anyway,"
he added. "Tell Stafford he's as unreliable as the reward of virtue. Coming,
Verny?" And they went out together.

Thayer sat as they had left him,
gazing into blankness. He was hardly
thinking. A terrible mental dumb-
ness comes to certain natures at times,
when the mind cannot tell to itself,
even, the cause of its pain. He had a
great craving for a pipe, but he was
the sort of a man who kept his word,
even to the detail of training. "The
game's up," he thought slowly, after
a little. "I've made failure of the
whole business, from start to finish.
If I could have only taken a decent

stand that would have been something, —but just to play a little foot ball, and to know enough to keep from getting dropped. Bah! Gray was right when he called me commonplace. I don't blame Stafford a bit for shaking me for somebody who knows something. Well, that's all over, and the best thing for me is to get myself out as soon as I can."

The shadow in the room had deepened into darkness. From his window Thayer could see in the rifts of the wind-swept clouds the gleam of the keen wintry stars.

Some one came up the stairs singing. Thayer recognized the voice as Stafford's. There came into the room a sudden brightness from the entry light outside, as he opened the door. "Is that you, Joe, in here in the dark?

Why the deuce don't you light up?"
he asked.

"Your gang has been here looking
for you," Thayer said, as he went over
to light his lamp.

"Who do you mean by that?"
asked Stafford. He was tearing up a
letter into minute square pieces.

"I mean," Thayer answered slowly,
"Gray, of course, and Ned Vernon.
Look here, Dick, the fellows are all
talking about it,—the way you are
running around with those chaps.
They think you're too good a man for
that sort of business. Why, those
men aren't ——"

The bits of paper had fluttered
down like a miniature momentary
snowstorm. "For gad's sake, Joe,
don't begin any of that cant about
Gray and Vernon. You can hold any

private opinion you like about them, only kindly remember, when you speak of them, that you are talking about my friends — my best friends."

Stafford picked up a book and turned over the leaves with elaborate carelessness. There was a moment's silence. Thayer pulled his cap down over his eyes and turned toward the door.

"You can have what friends you please — it's none of my business, of course," he said, as he went out.

Stafford went into his room to get ready for dinner. "I'll be hanged if I'll have him trying any missionary game on me," he said, half aloud. "If he did it because he cared a two-penny hurrah about me it would be different. But I object to being made an object of Christian Endeavor." He put out the lights and, going out, shut the door behind him as if he were venting a personal spite upon it.

Thayer had to be at the Gym. for signal practice for a while after he had finished dinner; and afterwards, instead of going back to his room, he stuffed his hands into his pockets and tramped off up Main street.

The moon had come up, and sometimes it peered out from behind scudding drifts of cloud for a moment, then drew back again as if afraid of what it had seen. A sharp wind from the north blew straight in Thayer's face. He hardly knew where he was going, or, indeed, how far he had gone. He met almost no one after he had gotten a little way out of the village, and the hills lay grim and silent in the darkness ahead of him.

He had come to the place where the road, leading down a sharp little hill, crosses a narrow bridge, and then mounts again to lose itself in a straggling pine wood. The moon had come out again and was sailing serenely through a stretch of starless blue.

Just as Thayer came to the little bridge some one entered it from the opposite side. " Gray ! " Thayer said.

Gray raised his head and saw him for the first time. " Yes," he said, doggedly, " perfect night for a walk isn't it ? "

Thayer did not seem to hear him. " For God's sake ! what's the matter? You look as if you'd seen a ghost."

" Your acumen does you credit," Gray said, in an echo of his old way of talking. " I have just been taking a promenade with one."

143

Thayer's impulse was to let him continue it uninterrupted. Conversation with Gray, under ordinary circumstances, was not an unmixed joy, and now he desired it less than ever. He started to pass on.

Gray had been watching him, and now moved toward him as if stirred by a sudden impulse. " Thayer," he said, in a curiously tense voice, and with a sort of desperate simplicity, " if I had been drowning in the water down there when you came by, would you have taken the trouble to pull me out?"

Thayer was silent a moment. " I suppose I would have," he said.

" Of course," Gray went on, quickly, " of course, I understand it would have been for purely impersonal reasons. Well, I'm drowning to-night, if

144

you only knew it. Will you help me, now?"

"Gray," said Thayer, harshly, "drop all this confounded mystery. What's the matter, in plain language?"

"But will you help me?" Gray persisted.

"I'll help you if I can," Thayer said, briefly; "you've got to tell me first."

Gray looked down into the rushing stream, clamoring below in the darkness.

"I'm not going in for an artistic statement," he began, slowly. "It's very simple. I had to have some money. I had no way of getting it, except one. I made out a check for the amount and wrote Ned Vernon's name on the back of it. Of course, I intended that it should be deposited again before he knew it. But I haven't been able to do it, and to-morrow, I have just found, that he's got to know all about it."

Thayer wanted to take the man by the throat. "You —— " he began, then breaking off with an effort he asked how great the amount was.

Gray laughed mirthlessly. " Not large enough to add the eclat of a magnificent recklessness, I'm afraid, or even to assure me a name with the mighty forgers of history. It was for a mere paltry one hundred and fifty dollars."

The sound of the rushing stream and of the wind in the pines filled the lonely silence. There was a momentary conflict going on in Thayer's right-angled brain. But only for a moment. Then he came to his conclusions quite calmly. Of course, he couldn't let this disgrace come to his friend's friend if he could prevent it. He scarcely considered Gray, his mind was so busy thinking of how he could save Stafford.

Presently he spoke. " Look here, Gray," he said, curtly, " I said I'd help you if I could, and I guess I can. I'll get you the money, and probably you'll be able to fix it up some way."

"Thayer, how can I ever thank you —" Gray began.

Thayer interrupted him. " Don't try to, for heaven's sake. You don't for a moment suppose it's for *you* that I'm doing it."

" Of course not," Gray said, almost humbly. " And if you tell Dick Stafford about all this ——"

" Do you think that I'm quite a

147

cad?" said Thayer, and they walked on in the darkness in silence.

Thayer was at his desk a day or so after writing a letter to his people. Letter writing amounted almost to a matter for fasting and prayer with Thayer at any time, and to-day it came harder than usual somehow. He was just finishing when Stafford came in.

He wandered about the room in an aimless fashion, when suddenly he said, " I've just heard that Bradford Gray's resigned from college."

Thayer bent lower over his desk. " Has he ? " he said.

Stafford hesitated for a moment, then he came over and put his hand on Thayer's shoulder. " Joe," he said, a little huskily, " he's told me the whole business. I wish I could tell you what I think of you, but I can't. Anyhow, I've been a fool — and worse — "

For answer, Thayer stretched out his hand, and in silence they both understood.

There are some things that are not for words, after all.

THE BOOTLICKING
OF BRONSON

The Bootlicking of Bronson.

EVERYBODY liked Jack Bronson. He was one of those men of whom we are accustomed to say that "they might amount to anything;" usually a euphemistic way of expressing the fact that, as yet, they amount to nothing. No one ever knew him to do or say anything especially brilliant, and yet he impressed you as being intensely clever. He was a tall youth, with a splendid pair of shoulders; his clothes were irreproachable, and he wore them with an air. I have seen Jack enter chapel in a sweater and rubber boots, and make the man who sat next to him, in all the glory of a high collar and black coat, look shabby by contrast.

But, after all, his distinguishing characteristic was his attitude toward work. I say attitude because no other word quite expresses it. Aversion would not do; he was not averse to it. But he seemed to live apart in a little world of his own, where work had not only no existence, but no possibility of existence.

Sometimes he studied, but always because he wanted to, not because he had to; and if you talked to him of the necessity of working harder he would answer you, politely indeed (Bronson was always polite), but with an air of boredom, mingled with a slightly suppressed impatience, very much as you might answer some ardent mathematician who tried to con-

vince you of the necessity of compre-
hending the fourth dimension.

How he ever stayed in college we
never discovered. Those who knew
him only slightly suggested that he
worked at night, when no one was
around; but his intimate friends rejected this explanation with scorn,
and attributed his continued residence
among us to the direct intervention of
Providence. He was usually either on
special probation, or out of college, or
just getting back again; and when he
had no condition to make up, which
happened but rarely, he was sure to
have extra work for over-cutting.

You would think that a life of such
uncertainty would have driven him
into nervous prostration ; on the contrary, he was the most cheerful man at
Williams. He continued his Damo-

155

clean existence during four unruffled years, and finally graduated, and had his degree framed and hung up in his room, where it remains to-day, the wonder and admiration of his friends.

But he frequently had narrow escapes, and this story is about one of them.

It was the spring term of Jack's Junior year, and he had been flunking steadily for three weeks. The Dean wrote to him, the professors exhorted him after class, the President himself, who knew his father, stopped him in the street to urge the necessity of reform. It was no use; the flunking continued. At last matters came to a crisis, and one morning Jack received a communication from the Secretary of the Faculty, informing him that, unless he passed a certain examination on the following Saturday, his "connection with the college," such was the wording of the note, "would at once and finally terminate."

Bronson did not take this very seriously. He handed the letter to a crowd of us at the post office and wandered leisurely up Spring street, merely remarking that he "guessed he'd get through all right." But we were less sanguine, and, after talking it over, several of us decided to try to arouse him to the gravity of the situation.

We found Bronson in his room smoking, and, after accepting his proffered tobacco, sat down and began to talk. We wanted to make an impression, and I think we talked steadily for nearly half an hour. When we were quite through Jack removed his pipe from his mouth and blew the smoke reflectively across the room.

"Really, fellows," he remarked, slowly, "I begin to think that I may be in some danger. After all, it is possible that the faculty intend to hold to that letter." We admitted that it was just possible.

"Well," he continued, "I don't see how I'm going to pass that exam Saturday. This is Tuesday, and I certainly can't do a whole term's work in three days." The moral was obvious; but no one ever thought of moralizing in connection with Bronson.

"Professor Parker is a good-natured chap," he went on thoughtfully, "May be if I bootlick him artistically he'll let me through. I believe I'll try it; it's my only chance, anyway." He paused a moment and then added po-

litely, " It's awfully good of you fellows to take this trouble for me."

We waived his thanks, and urged
him to brace up, and not trust to anything so unreliable as bootlicking.
"Oh, don't worry," he answered, " I'm
sure it will turn out all right." And
we had learned by experience that
when he made this remark there was
no use saying anything more.

The next morning it was pretty
well known throughout the class that
Jack Bronson was going to bootlick
Professor Parker. The news created
something of a sensation. That Jack
should exert himself sufficiently in the
interests of his education to bootlick
a member of the faculty, was regarded
as little short of marvelous. Then,
too, we felt sure that he would not
proceed according to the cut and dried

methods of ingratiation. We looked for something new and striking.

Professor Parker was a nice old man, with about as much of an idea of discipline as a six weeks' old kitten. One of those delightful, easy-going old gentlemen who are found on the faculty of every college in the country. Benevolence radiated from his entire person; kindliness was written in the lines of his wrinkled face, and every glance of his pleasant old eyes, and every tone of his quiet, leisurely voice, proclaimed a spirit of universal peace and good will.

He knew his subject thoroughly, and any one who was interested in the work could get a great deal from his course. If not, you simply loafed through the term, studied a couple of hours for the final, and then passed on a D minus. Sometimes the Professor conditioned a man, for form's sake, apparently, but he always let him through the make-up, not that he was too lazy to flunk him again, but simply because he was utterly incapable of inflicting pain on any one.

Naturally, Parker was very popular. His elective was filled to overflowing, and if many of us learned very little from our books, we learned something from contact with the man, that was, perhaps, quite as valuable to us as anything in the curriculum.

That morning he was even more easy-going than usual. He beamed upon us all as we came in, called a few men up, helped them out with their recitations good naturedly, and started on his lecture. He concluded it some fifteen minutes before the hour, and then, after reading the list of absences, proceeded to what he had evidently been looking forward to all through the recitation.

"For a long time," he began, "I have been planning an expedition to the old battlefield of Bennington. I am glad to say that at length the opportunity to visit it has come, and I would like very much to have any of you who care to go accompany me. We shall start this afternoon at five, spend the night at Bennington, and to-morrow drive out to the battlefield, which, as you know, is about seven miles from the town. I have always tried," he continued, "to awaken an interest in American history among the men who take this course, and if I have succeeded with any one of you, I think I can promise him a most interesting trip."

The Bootlicking of Bronson.

The Professor paused, and Bronson, who was sitting in the front row, said quietly : " I should be delighted to go with you, sir, if you care to have me."

We looked at each other significantly. Of course it was just what we had expected; and yet we felt slightly disappointed. You see, we had looked for something startlingly original from Jack, and this was, after all, only what any of us would have done under similar circumstances.

But when we suggested this to him after the recitation he withered us with a look of scorn. "Really!" said he, " I gave you credit for more discernment." We apologized meekly and he condescended to explain.

"You see what the whole trouble is, of course, don't you?" he asked. "You know Parker; he'd let me through in a minute if the rest of the faculty would let him. But they're dead onto him, and if he passes me they'll make him show them my paper, and then it's all up with little Willie. I've simply got to win his heart so completely that he'll refuse to let them see it, and stick by his refusal."

"Of course," he went on, noticing our incredulous air, "Of course I'm not going to trust entirely to my own personal charms. I may be conceited, but I hope I'm not quite so bad as that. But I have an idea. I can't tell you what it is just now; but if you want to find out come round to my room at half-past four." And he positively refused to tell us anything further.

Promptly at four-thirty we turned up at his room. Bronson was packing for the trip. His suit case lay open on the floor, and upon the divan was what looked like a very rusty old cannon ball. Some one started to lift it out of the way, but Jack stopped him. "Don't touch it," said he, "That is my idea." And then he explained the whole scheme to us.

"You see," he began, "I remember reading somewhere that every man had his weak point, and if you only knew what it was you could do anything you pleased with him. So I reflected that Parker's weak point was American history, and if I attacked him there I stood a good chance of winning.

"You will notice this object," indicating the ball with a wave of his hand. "Between you and me that is the old sixteen-pound shot that the athletic team used last October at the fall meet. They forgot to take it back to the Gym., and I saw it lying out on Weston Field one day, just before the Christmas vacation. As soon as Parker proposed the trip to Bennington I thought of this shot and went down to look for it. It was just where I had seen it last, and I carried it up here. Of course, it is very rusty, but that's all the better." He paused to light a cigarette, and then went on.

" Now, let me briefly outline our programme for to-night and to-morrow. We drive to Bennington and have dinner. After dinner I betray a deep interest in the battle, and, of course, Parker is delighted to tell me all about it. Well, we finally go to bed, and the next morning, just as we are starting out, I propose that we take a spade along and dig for relics. He approves of the scheme, and during the course of the day we discover the old Revolutionary cannon ball which you observe on the divan. We return in triumph, and I'll guarantee that Parker will resign from the faculty sooner than let me be dropped for flunking his exam."

We simply gasped. The magnitude of the plan fairly took our breath away. Bronson received our congratulations with modest pride, and asked us to help him pack.

But now an unlooked for difficulty presented itself. The ball was too large to go into the suit case Jack was in despair. "Haven't you a big valise?" suggested some one. "Yes, I know," he answered, disconsolately, "but I hate to carry a valise; it always

167

looks so sloppy." He really seemed quite distressed about it, but finally, with a sigh, he submitted to the inevitable.

Just as we finished packing, the Professor appeared in front of Morgan, seated in a broad, comfortable looking buckboard, that had done service on many similar expeditions.

"There he is," said Jack; "we mustn't keep him waiting. Have I everything packed? Let me see; shot at the bottom; heavy shoes; old golf suit; clean shirt and two extra collars; soap box, brushes, sponge and pajamas. Anything else? O, yes; my pipe!"

He put this last article in his pocket and went down stairs. From the window we saw him place the valise carefully under the seat and then clamber into the wagon himself. The Professor clucked to his horse, and the expedition to Bennington disappeared down the road.

If to be talked of is fame, Jack was famous that night. Nothing like this had ever been heard of in all the annals of bootlicking, and every one had something to say about it. Some predicted success; others, failure; but all agreed that the plan could only have originated with Jack Bronson.

We expected him back about nine o'clock Thursday evening, and a lot of us went up to his room to wait for him. However, it was almost ten before the sound of wheels on the driveway, followed by a loud "Whoa!" announced his return.

"Good night, Mr. Bronson," said the voice of Professor Parker (and as soon as he began to speak we could tell that he was fairly trembling with joyful excitement). "Good night, sir! Good night! This has been a most fortunate expedition; and its success is entirely due to you, for I should never have found it if you hadn't gone with me. Good night again!"

"Good night, Professor," answered Jack, and then we heard him coming up stairs. We rushed out and fell upon him in a body.

"Quick! Tell us about it! How did it turn out? Did he find it? Is he going to let you through? When ——"

"Shut up all of you!" answered Bronson, "or I'll go straight to bed without telling you a thing. Now then," he continued, as we stopped, utterly cowed by this threat; "first of all, has anyone something to eat? I'm half starved."

We gave him a box of crackers, and he ate them for what seemed an interminable time. Finally he finished, lit his pipe, leaned back in the most comfortable chair in the room, and began.

"Well, I had a splendid time. Parker is a great old boy, and he treated me so white that I felt ashamed of myself for fooling him. We didn't get to Bennington until quite late. It's a long drive anyway, and it's a good deal longer behind that horse of his. Really, though, the trip's worth taking; we had about the finest sunset last night that I ever saw; and if any of you are interested in scenery you want to —— "

But we were not interested in scenery, and said so. Jack looked at us reproachfully for a moment, and then

171

went on, exactly as though there had been no interruption.

" You want to take that drive before you graduate; it is really magnificent. We got there long after every one else was through dinner, and they had to cook one specially for us. But it was worth waiting for when it came. Yes," he repeated, thoughtfully, " It was worth waiting for.

" Then, after that, we sat out on the piazza, lit our pipes, and felt at peace with the world for half an hour. I tell you what, it was great, sitting there with a good dinner inside of you, and nothing to do but watch the smoke drift off through the dusk. I never felt more thoroughly comfortable in my life.

" By and by we began to talk, and

Parker told me a lot about Bennington, and drew a map of the battlefield on the floor of the piazza, which I copied for future use.

"The old buck really got eloquent. It seems that some relative of his commanded an American regiment, and you should have heard him describe the charge that won the victory. He talked so loud that one of the hotel people came out and asked him if he wanted anything, and then he laughed and sort of apologized to me for getting so excited.

"Finally, we went to bed, and when Parker wasn't looking I told the clerk to have me waked at half-past five.

"Next morning I got up, took a cold tub and came down stairs, feeling like a prince. I went round to the livery stable and asked them for the best horse they had, and they gave me a little mare who hadn't been out for three days, so they said. She took those fourteen miles as if they were nothing at all, and I got back long before eight with the shot nicely planted in the spot where the regiment of Parker's ancestor had stood. I located the place pretty nearly from the map.

"When I reached to the hotel the old gentleman was just coming down stairs. He complimented me on my early rising, and asked me what I had been doing. I told him that I had been looking around a little, which was more or less true, and we went in to breakfast. By the way, if any of you ever go to Bennington you want to stop at that hotel; their cooking is excellent, and they have an awfully pretty waitress.

The Bootlicking of Bronson.

"After breakfast we got them to put up a lunch for us and started off for an all day trip to the battlefield. When I suggested taking a spade along he wasn't very enthusiastic, for he said the whole field had been dug over for relics twenty times before. But I told him we might happen to find something, and that, at any rate, I would do all the digging.

"I intended to save the cannon ball for the afternoon, so we spent the morning wandering around the place, while Parker turned himself into a guide book. He got even more excited than he had the night before, and ranged over the field like an old war horse. It really was great to listen to him, and he knows an awful lot about the Revolution.

"You ought to have seen me do the

deeply-interested act. I simply laid myself out to be agreeable, and agreed with all his pet theories respectfully. Then he switched off from the Revolution and began to lecture me on my low stand. I took it all in without a smile, and promised to try to be a good boy in the future. When he finally wound up his discourse we were both ready for something to eat.

"We ate our lunch under some trees and lay in the shade, smoking and loafing until about three. Then I said I thought I'd dig for relics, and he laughed and answered, 'All right, go ahead,' he would take a nap. So I got him to point out what he thought was a likely place, and dug around for over half an hour. Of course, I could simply have gone straight for the shot, but I wanted to do the job up artistically.

The Bootlicking of Bronson.

" Well, after I had excavated a small cellar and was feeling pretty tired, I thought it was about time to work up to the climax. So I went over to the Professor and told him I was going to try the place where the regiment of the original Parker had stood. He got quite interested at that, and said he 'guessed he'd come and watch me.'

" I started about eight feet from the shot and dug straight towards it. When I got pretty close, Parker asked if I didn't want him to take a turn. I had intended to find the 'relic' myself, but, of course, I saw at once how much better it was to let him do it, so I gave him the spade and sat down to wait for developments.

" He dug for a minute or two, and then I saw him drop down on his knees and begin to scrape around in the dirt with his hands. Suddenly he gave a yell like an Indian.

"'What's the matter?' said I, innocently.

"'Matter!' he cried, and I swear the old fellow was almost crying from pure joy; 'Matter!' he lifted out the shot and held it up triumphantly!

"'Do you know what this is?' he asked.

"I did, but I thought I'd better not tell him.

"'No,' said I, 'I don't.'

"His voice sank into an awed whisper.

"'It's a cannon ball,' said he; 'found in the exact spot where my ancestor stood! Perhaps it was fired at his very regiment! Mr. Bronson, this is a most priceless relic of the Revolution!'

"Well, naturally, I was all sympathetic enthusiasm in a minute. He gloated over that shot as though it had been a gold nugget, and would hardly let me carry it for him. Then, of course, everybody at the hotel had to hear about it; and you should have seen him standing there, beaming away, while they all congratulated him.

"Finally we got started for home, and he talked a steady stream all the way back, and thanked me over and over again for going with him. Doubtless you witnessed from the window our affecting good nights.

"That's all there is to tell, except that I'll bet four to one with any man here that I pass that exam."

But not even the most reckless of us would take him up.

The Bootlicking of Bronson.

The next day Professor Parker brought the shot into the class-room, and we listened with much outward gravity to the description of its discovery. Only once did we come near breaking down, and that was when the good Professor remarked innocently:

"I am unable as yet to discover the significance of the lettering on the ball — 'W. & D., Boston' — but I presume that 'W. & D.' may be the initials of the company who made it."

Subsequently the "relic" was placed in Clark Hall, and, after a considerable portion of the college had viewed it, the manager of the athletic team wrote to Professor Parker, explaining the situation, and asking him to return the shot.

It was returned.

But long before that happened Bronson had passed his examination.

HIS FIRST RUSH

181

His First Rush.

M RS. KENDALL'S devotion to
her son amounted almost to a
religion. It was delightful in theory,
but rather a mingled blessing in practice, and Mr. Kendall, who for some
years had viewed, with increasing
anxiety, the development of his off-
spring's character in the hothouse
atmosphere of motherly solicitude,
decided that it was time to interfere,
if Percy was ever going to amount
to anything. College was the readiest
solution of the question, and Williamstown was two hundred miles
from New York and the maternal cod-
dling; he decided to send Percy to
Williams.

Mrs. Kendall, who was, after all, a sensible woman if rather a foolish mother, acquiesced in her husband's decision after some opposition, and went up to Williamstown the next fall to see Percy settled in his new quarters; somehow it never occurred to her that he was capable of attending to the settling process himself.

They stayed at the Greylock, and were very pleasantly surprised, when they came downstairs on the evening of their arrival, to find Mrs. Armitage and her daughter in the dining room. Now Percy liked Louise Armitage very much, and the month they had spent together at Lakewood the winter before furnished them with abundant topics for conversation.

"I wish you were going to be there this winter," she said, as they were sitting after dinner in one of the little parlors; "but I suppose you are a fixture in Williamstown for some time to come. Do you remember the long inclosed piazzas at the Laurel House, and the conservatory with all those queer-looking palms?"

"Of course I do," answered Kendall, "and the artificial lake and the trees with the long moss hanging from them. But I am afraid this is the last chance that I will have to see you until next summer. When do you leave here?"

"Oh, not for a week. Mamma has an idea that the climate agrees with her; it's rather dull for me, though, for I really don't know any one here well except Jack Updyke. He's in college, you know."

"Yes; a junior, isn't he?"

"I believe so; anyway he's been awfully nice. He said he was coming up to the dance to-night."

"Do they dance here?" asked Percy.

"Oh, yes, every evening. It's splendid, there are so many men. Quite a contrast to the usual summer hotel, isn't it? But they're all sort of alike, and what's worse, they all say the same things. I've really got tired of telling them how fine the scenery is, and I don't dare ask them too much about the college, because there are such lots of things here one musn't talk about at all. It's very puzzling sometimes, but I suppose it doesn't seem so to them. Still I wish —" But just then the music began in the ballroom and Louise departed in search of her mother.

186

Thus it came about that when Jack Updyke reached the hotel that evening, the first person he saw was Kendall dancing with Miss Armitage, in blissful ignorance of the scandalized looks of the upper classmen present.

"How does that strike you for freshness?" said one of them to Jack as he came in, "he's been dancing here for twenty minutes and he won't leave that girl long enough to give us a chance to call him down."

Updyke was rather amused to hear the meek, ladylike, be-mothered Percy called fresh. "I don't believe he understands," said he, "I'll speak to him myself."

And, being a person of considerable tact, he crossed the floor, greeted Mrs. Kendall effusively, insisted on taking Percy off with him to see his room,

and had him half way down Main
street before he had a chance to
object. Then Updyke walked him
around for half an hour and told
him things. Kendall listened with a
growing bewilderment.

"But how was I to know that freshmen weren't allowed to dance at the
Hotel?" he protested; "I suppose
I've got all those fellows down on
me?"

"Oh it's not quite so bad as that,"
said Jack, laughing, "but you see
there are a lot of things that a man
has to be careful of when he first
comes here, if he doesn't want to queer
himself." And then he preached to·
Kendall the great doctrine of college
custom, which seems so foolish to
the outsider, and so vital to the
undergraduate.

If Percy had not been an exceedingly meek individual he would probably have resented Updyke's patronage, for they were about of an age; but instead, he thanked him humbly and returned to the Greylock, to parry as well as he could his mother's inquiries as to what he had been doing.

During the next few days he was pretty well occupied. He bought furniture, saw the Registrar, attended his first recitations, and incidentally met a good many of his class. His mother left the day college opened, and Percy missed her more than he had expected to; but he was too busy to feel homesick just yet,— that came later.

He was sitting in his room one afternoon when there was a knock at the door, and Updyke came in.

"I thought I'd stop for you," he said; "all ready for the ball game?"

"I don't understand," answered Kendall; "what ball game?"

Updyke whistled. "Really, my dear Percy," said he, "pardon me, but you need a nurse. Don't you know that the annual freshman-sophomore base ball game, with its attendant rush, occurs this afternoon?"

"I heard something about it," replied Kendall, "but I thought I wouldn't go. I don't play base ball, you know."

"So I imagined; but unless you want to be queered from one end of Main street to the other you'd better hustle right down to Weston Field this afternoon and lay for sophomores. The man who cuts this rush is apt to get himself disliked."

His First Rush.

"O, I don't want to get out of the rush," answered Percy hastily; and to do him justice he didn't. "Just wait until I change my clothes, will you? I suppose I'd better wear a sweater."

"It's just as well to," answered Updyke; "a high collar is apt to be awkward in a rush."

Kendall went into his bedroom and returned with a pair of worn-out trousers. 'I brought these with me on purpose," he remarked, holding them up for inspection.

Updyke smiled; he had done exactly the same thing himself freshman year. "You certainly can't hurt them," he replied, non-committally.

The other went on with his preparations; evidently he had thought them all out before. He put on the trousers, fastened them with a disreputable belt, and then, having donned his sweater and slipped on a very ancient coat, stood up with the air of one who has made up his mind to face what must be faced cheerfully. "I'm all ready," he announced.

Updyke laughed outright. "You talk as if you were going to war," said he; "it's only a ball game."

Percy colored. "But there'll be a rush, won't there?" he asked defensively.

"Yes," answered the junior, "but a rush isn't such a very serious affair after all." He looked out of the window. "The fellows seem to be going down," said he; "suppose we start."

The two went down stairs, Kendall carefully locking his study door, after the manner of freshmen during the first few weeks of the fall term. On the way Updyke proceeded to tell his companion something about the nature of the afternoon's amusement.

"You see," he explained, "the game is only a fake; the sophomores almost always win; the main thing is the rush, and the fun that the seniors have with the freshmen. You'd better stick close to your class, and don't make yourself any more prominent than you can help, or you may get into trouble. There go some fellows I want to speak to," he added, as a group of juniors passed by on the other side of the street; "I'll see you later. Good-bye," and he was gone.

Kendall walked on alone, hoping that he didn't look as nervous as he felt. The first weeks of college are rather bewildering, and he lived in a

193

state of constant apprehension, for fear he should do something to queer himself; for Jack had not failed to impress upon him the vast number of ways by which a freshman may accomplish that deplorable result.

Just at present, however, he was chiefly concerned about the rush; he wondered what it would be like, and whether there was much chance of his getting badly hurt. Various stories that he had heard at home recurred unpleasantly to his mind. At any rate he was in for it now, and he might just as well make the best of things. After all it would be something to talk of. A rush was only a rush, and he was a fool to be so frightened about it.

"Oh, Fresh!"

Percy jumped as if he had been shot, and a party of sophomores just

behind burst into a roar of laughter
and, hustling him out of the way, went
on down the street. Blushing furi-
ously, and trying to look as if he didn't
know it, he started to walk on, when
he was hailed by a man in his own class,
whom he knew slightly.

" Hello, Kendall ! Going to the
game ? "

" Yes," he answered, and the two
went down together.

Weston Field presented quite a fes-
tive appearance. Almost the whole
college was there. Between home and
first base the sophomores were lined
up in a solid body, and their yell rang
out at intervals, sharp and distinct, in
marked contrast to the straggling cheer
that came from the crowd of freshmen,
gathered between home and third.
The upper classmen were seated in the

grand stand, and quite a number of visitors had come to look on, most of them in carriages of one sort or another. Presently a coach came through the rustic entrance gate with a great blowing of horns and, bowling up the field at a fast trot, swung into position on the east side of the diamond.

There was some delay in starting the game, but at last the umpire called the two captains to him and tossed up a coin. The sophomore glanced at it and nodded to his class, who cheered vigorously; a moment later the team trotted out to their positions, the freshman batter took his place, and the game began.

As the first ball pitched struck the catcher's mitt, the upper classmen commenced to pour out of the grand stand, the juniors going among the freshmen to encourage them to deeds of violence, while the seniors gathered on one side of the field and consulted together with great animation.

The man at the bat was a loosely-built youth, with very red cheeks, whose color was considerably heightened by the extremely personal comments showered upon him by the sophomores. They ranged from allusions to his personal appearance to remarks on the utter impossibility of his hitting the ball. He was badly rattled even before the game actually began, and when the pitcher craftily threw the first ball straight for his head, so that he only saved himself by a quick dodge, it destroyed his small remnant of self-possession. He hit wildly at three distant outs and retired, amid the triumphant jeers of the entire sophomore class.

The next man was of a different sort. He took his place quickly, and pounded the plate confidently with his bat, quite undisturbed by shouts of " How well he does it!" "Where did you get that shape?" " I can't keep my eyes off your feet," and similar specimens of sophomoric wit. He let the first ball go by, and, when the next came, knocked a neat single just over the short-stop's head. The freshmen cheered, the sophomores groaned, the fielder ran wildly after the ball, and the umpire called safe.

But the man who followed him went out on a little pop fly to the infield, and his successor sent a grounder straight into the first base-man's hands.

His First Rush.

The sophomores came in for their half of the inning, and the freshmen, aided and abetted by the juniors, grew eloquent in their denunciation of the batters, for in this game all the usual rules of procedure are laid aside; a freshman may, without reproach, make himself conspicuous by loud conversation, and the cheering of errors is, on that day, and on that day only, countenanced on Weston Field.

Two innings went by without either side having scored, and the third was just beginning when Kendall felt himself pushed violently to one side by a sudden movement of the crowd. The cause of the disturbance was a long line of seniors marching in single file, with their hands on each other's shoulders.

They went straight for the home

plate, everybody hastily making way
for them, and walked solemnly around
the diamond, while the game stopped,
and the players waited for further developments. Suddenly they rushed
into the crowd and returned, bearing
in their midst three hapless freshmen,
who were soon standing, hat in hand,
making trembling speeches to their
captors.

When their eloquence was exhausted
the seniors sought other victims, and
the ball game speedily degenerated
into a wholly transparent excuse for
horse play. They placed the batter
on the scorer's table, and shouted with
glee when he swung at the ball and
fell off; they took up the bases, and
substituted instead three men standing on all fours; they called upon the
outfielders for "a few remarks on the

game," and would not be denied, and, finally, they retired behind the grand stand, where a quartet of freshmen sang for their edification.

All this time the two under classes had gradually been growing more and more violent in their mutual abuse. They howled and yelled in wild attempts to drown each other's cheers. To the derisive cry of "Oh, Fresh!" the freshmen responded by an equally scornful shout of "Oh, Sophs!" and although these expressions appear innocent enough, they had a very irritating effect on both parties. A belligerent sophomore called loudly on his class to "Rush those freshmen off the field," and his advice seemed to find favor with them, in spite of the defiant "Don't you wish you could?" that greeted it.

Kendall felt that matters were coming to a crisis, and, stuffing his cap under his sweater to keep it from being lost, prepared for battle.

Now the juniors came to the fore, and with shouts of "Close up!" "Bunch together there!" formed the freshmen into a compact body, with the largest men in front. Then one of them, who had thoughtfully stolen a sophomore sweater earlier in the afternoon, handed it to a man in the center of the mass, with instructions to wave it upside down when the proper moment came.

Everything now being ready, the sweater was elevated on high, amid loud cheers from the freshmen, and cries of "Oh, Sophs, are you going to stand that?" from the upper classes. Evidently the sophomores were not;

they gathered together in close order, and came rushing across the field. Kendall, who somewhat against his will, found himself in the front rank, wondered vaguely what was going to happen to him when the crash came, but he really didn't have time to be very much frightened. The green strip of grass between the classes narrowed rapidly; the flushed, excited faces of the advancing sophomores glared close into his; there was a great heave of the mass behind him, and the rest was blind, suffocating, intolerable pressure, with a man striking at his head.

The front ranks of both parties were lifted off their feet by the force of the encounter, and held there; when they came to earth again the rush had resolved itself into a confused mass of

struggling men, in the midst of which
was the sweater. Those near it fought
savagely for its possession, and the
men on the outside took long running dives and clambered recklessly
over the heads of the crowd to join in
the main battle that raged in the
center. Some fell down and the rest
fought over them, which is not so dangerous as it sounds, because, if one
is careful to protect his head, and
watches a favorable chance to clamber
up by the legs of those around him, he
may escape with very little damage.

A rush is too violent a form of exercise to last very long, and this one
ceased as suddenly as it had begun.
The solid mass broke into struggling
segments; these, in turn, split into little groups of three or four men; the
upper classmen ran in and pulled

these groups apart and behold it was all over.

Percy found himself with a torn coat and a very black eye, standing with one foot through a derby that some one had been foolish enough to wear, while Updyke grinned at him cheerfully.

"Feel used up?" he inquired.

"A little," answered Kendall, and in fact he felt very much used up indeed. He sat down to get his breath again, and the process took longer than he expected, for most of it had been driven forcibly out of him. Just as he was beginning to feel better some seniors came along. escorting two very scared looking men.

"Here's the freshman who danced at the hotel," called one, noticing Kendall sitting there; "let's bring him along, too."

Percy remembered what followed as one remembers a bad dream. The seniors led their victims in front of one of the carriages at the edge of the field, and made them dance for the amusement of its occupants. He was too conscious of the very absurd figure he must cut to dare to lift his eyes from the ground until the performance was over; and when he did so he wanted nothing so much as a place to hide in. For there on the front seat, laughing quite as heartily as any one, sat Louise Armitage.

He called on her that evening. He felt that matters couldn't possibly be made any worse than they were, and she was going away the next morning. So he appeared at the hotel, black eye and all, and found her in.

" I hope you have enjoyed your

visit here," he said, as he shook hands with her. "At any rate, you'll have an awfully good story to tell about me."

But Louise was a very nice girl, and, moreover, she liked Percy.

"No," she answered, "I don't think I will. You know I said that there were some things here one mustn't talk about at all — well, this is one of them."

TEMPORA MUTANTUR

209

Tempora Mutantur.

IF there is one time in all the year when one can call himself most fortunate in being a Williams man and an undergraduate, it is during the last two or three days of May. For most it is a time of pure carelessness and enjoyment.

To be sure, those who set their happiness on being somebody and figuring in a prominent position in college, are apt to have work enough and worry enough. For instance, if you are a sophomore and of this ilk, you will be chosen, perhaps, on the Prom. committee, and then you will find yourself no end busy with the thousand and one arrangements connected with the dance — pillaging your friends' rooms for decorations for the Gym.; receiving the palms and other potted plants that come up from Troy, and tending to numberless other details. Perhaps you have dramatic talent and are cast for the comedy which " Cap and Bells " is to give, and then, of course, you can have no thought for anything else. Or, possibly, you may be the manager of the base ball team and have the grave responsibility on your shoulders of winning the Decoration Day game and of providing good weather there-for. But supposing you are none of these, only an ordinary undergradu-ate, without ambitions for collegiate distinction — or, at least, ambitions which have materialized — you can have a most thoroughly good time.

Tempora Mutantur.

For two or three days you have very little to do with your books. There are recitations and lectures, of course, except on the Thirtieth, and it is just as well to go to them if you are short of cuts and have no other engagements; but preparation is hardly expected and quite out of the question, anyway. Even the most abandoned grinds allow the dust to collect on their desks — nor, if scientific, do the Labs. see them for forty-eight hours together — while they sally forth in ducks and négligé shirts to track meets or tennis games, or mayhap to no more profitable occupation than mere idle saunterings and smokings on the soft new grass, with a neglect that is shocking of precious time and patent opportunities.

The latter part of May is the play-day season of the year. You can stand in the middle of Main street and look in either direction under the arch of the trees, into a very paradise of new verdure — and with more or less of a belief in earthly paradises, too. Summer is just in the first triumphant flush of her youth. The sky is soft and blue, the air mild, and the Berkshires stand clad in a green seductiveness that is a thousand times more fetching than the vaunted splendors of their autumn attire. Very commonplace things are these, blue sky and green hills; but they do not seem commonplace when the recollection is still fresh of the long winter, or when you have not yet forgotten the rain and the chill and the mud of that interregnum of anarchy between a New England winter and summer, which is charitably called spring.

Tempora Mutantur.

And then there is more color about the streets than at other times, and a few soprano voices can be heard in chapel mingled with the accustomed masculine bass, when the hymn is sung. Williams entertains friends from sister colleges, and from the neighboring cities, after the long months of hibernation.

They begin to come a day or two before the festivities commence, and are shown about the town and the college buildings or taken to drive out in the country. They are conscious of being favored guests, and the happy interest they take in everything is infectious. Many a man becomes quite enthusiastic in pointing out, among the treasures of Clark Hall, the priceless jaw bone of some ancient geological unpronounceable, and explaining how desirous was the curator of such and such a museum to get that jaw bone at any cost, and how his tenders had been rejected; or on showing the other objects of interest connected with his Alma Mater — the existence of which, in all probability, he had been quite ignorant of, until, out of the necessity of playing the cicerone, came some slight knowledge of the place he had been living in for several years.

A great shout of triumph went up when the last man crossed the plate, bringing to an end the wild cheering which had continued without pause throughout the last three innings. The game was over — the Decoration Day game, which is the base ball game of the year. It had taken twelve in-

nings to finish it, but it had ended
finally in a victory for the home team.
This was in keeping with the old es-
tablished custom of the college, " re-
nowned for base ball and free trade,"
that there should be on Decoration
Day a close game, and yet one that
should terminate in victory.

Consequently every one was hila-
riously, even frantically, happy and
patriotic. Confusion reigned on the
field. The players, with bat bags and
sweaters under their arms, ran for the
barges which were to take them to
the Gymnasium, or were carried there
on the shoulders of enthusiastic ad-
mirers. The gate was choked with
coaches and drags, crowded with girls
wearing purple ribbons or carrying
flags with the " W " on them. The
masses on foot who had stood along

the ropes and borne the brunt of the cheering fell in behind the vehicles, hoarse and weary, but none the less enthusiastic, and tramped up through the village, singing, " We want those streets all paved with purple, royal purple," and the other familiar snatches of doggerel through which the Williams undergraduate gives vent to his feelings in times of high pressure.

The crowd gathered on the terrace at the east end of Morgan, dusty and perspiring, and there the singing was continued in better form. Then Dr. Dane, one of the " Kid Faculty " and not over-popular, was seen crossing Main street, and immediately a committee waited upon him with an urgent request for a speech. The doctor came up on the sidewalk before the crowd, said as many pleasant and congratulatory things as he could think of impromptu, and was sent away with a cheer that was more good-natured than the one that had ended the serenade he had been favored with not many weeks before.

Next Jack French, who had captained the team to victory in the early nineties, was pounced upon and made to prophesy on the chances for a championship that season. Then there were cheers for the team as a whole, and cheers for each member of the team individually, and for the Amherst players as they came out of the Gym. and scrambled into their barge. One can do a great deal of cheering on Decoration Day after a victory without having it seem to get monotonous.

By this time the crowds were beginning to gather in front of the Labs. to

watch the election of the juniors to the
Gargoyle Society. Already several
men were sitting on Thompson perch,
and the rest came by twos and threes
till the whole junior class was
assembled.

There were some men, of course,
who felt sure they would be pulled off
the fence — the captains and managers
of the athletic teams and those at the
head of the other organizations — and
there were others who were equally
certain that they would not be, but
there still remained not a few whose
fate hung in the balance, so that quite
a number of men in the long line found
it difficult to maintain the appearance
of indifference they considered required of them.

Bigelow, of the senior class, stood
over by Kellogg, with his room-mate's

mother and Miss Blodgett, waiting for the election to begin. Bob Spaulding was a junior, and consequently had to be with his class on the perch. Bigelow had just been explaining to Miss Blodgett the way in which the men were chosen.

" But what sort of a society is it, Mr. Bigelow?" she asked. " I have heard Bob speak of the Gargoyle often enough, but I never asked him to explain what it was. He talks about so many college things I don't know about."

" It's rather hard to classify as an organization, I should say," Bigelow replied. " Perhaps one might call it a mutual admiration society."

" No, but what do they do when they get elected with all this fuss?" the girl persisted.

"Why, in the first place, they have a banquet, and then they hold secret meetings every little while and talk a great deal at them, I understand, and when the faculty endangers the stability or the good name of the college by any rash act, they come to the rescue. Now, you have it all, I believe, that is, as well as an outsider can give it to you."

"You are joking with me; you college men can never be serious," the girl said petulantly. "I wish you would tell me. But I believe you are 'sore'—that's the word, isn't it—because you weren't elected last year."

That was the word, but it made Bigelow wince to hear a girl use it.

"That remark does more credit to your penetration, Miss Blodgett, than to your charity," he answered. "I shall have to be more careful in future and not disclose any more of my weaknesses to you."

After a day or two's acquaintance with his friend's fiancée, Bigelow had come to the conclusion that he rather liked her, in spite of — but Bigelow's likes were usually qualified by a rather, before, and an in spite of, after them. The girl was certainly different from the average, and she interested him as a type. Then she was pretty — decidedly pretty, and that covers a multitude of defects in a casual acquaintance. Still, Bigelow rather wondered why Bob should have got engaged to her. But he did not worry about this. The engagement had lasted ever since the time Bob had entered college, and she probably suited him. Bigelow had always the comfortable consciousness that all men were not so fastidious as he; and that, in measuring most things, it was necessary to subtract something from his own standards in order to get normal results.

"Ah, there they come at last," he said.

The twenty seniors forming the Gargoyle Society had just come in sight beyond Kellogg. They were walking slowly, two by two, dressed in their caps and gowns. The procession came down the path that leads across the campus to the Laboratories, and then turned off to the left and formed a circle on the grass.

"I want to laugh," said the girl, "but I suppose I shouldn't. It looks just like an Odd Fellows' funeral, only solemner."

When the circle was formed, one

gowned figure left the others, and, walking out to the path, made a square military turn, and then went down to the fence, where another turn was executed. Then he walked with measured strides along the line of expectant juniors.

"That's Kendrick, president of the Gargoyle," Bigelow explained. "He chooses the first man as he comes back."

Kendrick reached the end of the fence, faced about and walked slowly back, scanning the row of attentive faces. Halfway down the line he stopped and extended his hand to one of the men on the fence, who slipped from his seat at once and was conducted with head uncovered to the circle of seniors, while his classmates and the spectators applauded.

"That's Judson, captain of the foot

ball team," said Bigelow. "Everyone knew he would make it."

Another Gargoyle left the circle, went through the same elaborate manœuvres and returned with a second junior. It was the manager of the next year's base ball team that was chosen. Then followed the president of the Y. M. C. A., the editor of the Gul., and the captains and managers of the other teams. At first there was no very great interest in the election. These men, from the offices they held, were practically sure of it. But as the number of chances decreased and the doubtful men began to be chosen, there was considerable suppressed excitement among the juniors and in the crowd of spectators.

"Who is that?" Miss Blodgett asked. "I danced with him last night in the Gymnasium, but I've forgotten his name."

"Harper. He's one of Bob's quite intimate friends."

"I don't like him," she said decisively.

Mrs. Spaulding gave the girl a deprecatory glance. "Why, Margery, I thought he was a very pleasant young man when Rob introduced him to me at the hotel."

Mrs. Spaulding had taken no part in the conversation up to this time. The caste of age is very strong with people who have lived all their lives in country towns, and she evidently thought it would be an unpardonable intrusion for a middle-aged matron to mingle in the talk of young people. This attitude amused Bigelow not a little.

There remained three men to be

chosen. Bigelow was beginning to feel uneasy about his friend's chances. Bob had played on the foot ball team for three years at center, and had been one of the most faithful workers — never brilliant, but steady, and always to be depended upon, and Bigelow had hoped that he would make it.

The next choice put his fears to rest. The eighteenth man stopped before Spaulding, and led him to the circle now almost complete. The applause, which had become rather perfunctory as time went on, was loud and hearty as Bob Spaulding's six feet two slipped off the fence, for Bob was one of the most popular men in the class, and had not an enemy in college.

" I'm afraid Bob's head will be turned by such an ovation," Miss Blodgett remarked.

She had said it laughingly, but there was something in the tone which made Bigelow look up at her quickly.

"You must give him a lesson if he gets to putting on airs, Miss Blodgett," he said gravely.

"If I can — but, perhaps that isn't so easy as it sounds," she answered gaily. "But I'll try, I assure you, if his vanity gets too insufferable."

The twentieth man had just been led within the circle of seniors, and now they all began marching away in double file, each senior leading the man he had chosen. The procession came up the path, around in front of Kellogg, and down the driveway before Morgan. They stopped under the stone gargoyle, which is over the further of the two north entrances of the building, and Kendrick stepped out from the others.

"Now, fellows, the old yell for the senior Gargoyle," he said.

'Rah! rah! rah! Willyums, yams, yums, Willyums, Ninety ———," the juniors shouted.

"And now for next year's Gargoyle," said Kendrick.

The cheer was repeated, with the numerals of the junior class at the end.

"And now one for the college."

The yell was given again and the crowd separated.

Bob Spaulding hastened over to the sidewalk where his friends were waiting. On the way he was stopped a dozen times by men who were eager to congratulate him. Bob's election was a surprise to him, for he had always been inclined to underrate his own importance on the team and in college, and the general approval which it called forth gave him a great deal of pleasure.

The sun had just gone down as they walked up Main street to the Greylock, and above the green bank of the Petersburg range the sky was a dull red. A quiet reigned in the broad elm-shaded street that was very agreeable, after the excitement and commotion of the afternoon. People were wending their way supperward in all directions.

Bob walked with his mother. They had just turned into the long shady path that leads from West up to the end of the street. Margery was a little way ahead of them with Bigelow.

Bob could see that people turned to look at her in admiration. He was aware of the fact that wherever he had

231

taken her during the last two or three days she had attracted attention, just as half his friends had fallen in love with the photographs he had of her in his room. He remembered the feeling of pleasure and pride it had given him to notice the covert glances which the early acquaintances of his freshman year had bestowed upon the picture of her that stood on his desk.

For some reason he did not have that sort of feeling now. To tell the truth, though he had never admitted it, even to himself, he had hoped, all along, that something would happen to prevent the visit that Margery and his mother had planned. He did not know why, or would not, for he had never allowed the thought to remain long enough in his mind to analyze it. It was a fear, only, that in some way she would not be all that he might wish her to be, or that he once thought her to be.

He had always combatted the fear, despising himself for having to combat it, just as now he was engaged in the same sort of honorless fight with what struggled in his consciousness to be recognized as the realization of it. These sneaking, disloyal thoughts were a new thing to Bob Spaulding, and he did not know how to deal with them. He could not be brutally truthful with himself without regard for consequences, as Bigelow always was.

With a mother's intuition Mrs. Spaulding had guessed what was in Bob's mind — at least partially — in the last few days. She watched him as he walked on in silence beside her.

"Has there been any misunderstanding between you and Margery, Robert?" she ventured.

Bob looked up quickly.

"No, mother. What made you think so? Madge and I are as good friends as ever, I guess." He was startled that the question should strike as closely as it did.

"Good friends, Robert; you should be more than good friends." She paused for a moment. "Since I have been here I have thought that you and Margery haven't the same feeling for one another as you used to have. Don't think that I am reproaching you, Robert, but I can't help seeing that you have changed in more than one way — it's quite natural that you should. But remember, if it is true that you do not love Margery ——"

"But it's not true, mother," Bob burst out impatiently; "you're all wrong."

They walked the rest of the way in silence.

She detained him a moment as he turned to leave her on the veranda of the hotel. "I don't believe my boy will ever lose his love for his father and mother, even if he does give up their old-fashioned ways," she said. "I didn't mean you to think that, Robert."

Bob was sitting with the rest of his class in Prof. Harvey's lecture room. The festivities of the Thirtieth were past, the visitors from out of town had gone away, and the college had settled down to its routine of work and play. Bob had been restless and dissatisfied

with himself ever since his mother and
Margery had gone home. This morning he was especially uneasy and would
have cut, except that his limit of absences had already been passed some
time before, and the number of over-
cuts increasing ominously.

At first he made an attempt to take
notes, writing down quite at random,
and without the slightest regard for
logical sequence, whatever seemed like
an important statement in the professor's lecture. This was Bob's usual
method of taking notes; and why he
took them at all was a mystery, which
he would have found it hard to explain
very satisfactorily. He never thought
of looking at them again, for when examination came he always borrowed
some one else's note book. Still a
vague sense of duty made him fill a

book with something or other for each of his lecture courses.

This morning it was harder than usual to follow, with even tolerable understanding, the professor's discourse. Bob gave it up at last, and began looking out of the window. Presently the Gym. clock struck the three-quarters. Bob sighed wearily. That meant forty-five minutes more, unless Teddy should relent and let them out early.

Then, for the want of something better to do, he began to observe what was going on in the room. His seat in the back row commanded a good view.

A little further along, on the same line of seats with him, Billy White and Guy McLane were playing tit-tat-toe on the fly leaf of a text book, and indulging in suppressed giggles, in a manner worthy of sixteen-year-old school girls. In another direction Caverly Harper was reading a yellow-covered novel, and taking no pains that Prof. Harvey should not notice his inattention either. Caverly was always frank to a degree in his attitude toward his instructors. Not far away Markham was composing some verses to a real or imaginary Marjorie, which would probably appear among the Cobwebs in the next Weekly.

To be sure, there were some men who were evidently following the lecture with interest — more in fact than Bob would have said, had he been asked, but they did not form a large majority. A good many had note books in which they scribbled, listlessly, when there was nothing to distract their attention elsewhere; and

238

not a few were sitting with vacant faces diddling their pencils and thinking of Heaven knows what, certainly not of Teddy's lecture. In the very front row was Fred Knowles, with his head on his arm, apparently asleep. Yet in spite of this there was no diminution in the earnestness of the professor's manner.

What a farce it all was. Bob had been attending just such exercises now for almost three years, and until this morning it had never struck him that there was anything peculiar about them. It had been a matter of course that in certain required subjects one should go to lectures every day, pay as little attention to them as possible, and, when examination time came, cram enough from a syllabus the night before to get through.

239

At last the hour was over. Bob lit his pipe, as usual, in the little niche in the doorway of Hopkins, and strolled down Spring street to Watson's, and loafed about there for a while. Some one asked him to play pool but he refused, without giving any reason, and started for his room in Kellogg, with the rather vague purpose of looking over some German for an afternoon quiz.

He found Bigelow there, stretched out on the divan in an exasperatingly comfortable, contented manner, reading a volume of French poetry.

Bob did not find his German book in the bookcase, and began overhauling the papers and magazines on the center table, with a great to do. Bigelow watched him placidly.

The search proved vain. Bob began walking about the room.

"Look here, Dud," he broke out suddenly, "I wish you would tell me why the hell I came to college, any-way."

Bigelow looked at him with amuse-ment. "Why, what's wrong with the place, Bob?" he asked. "I always considered you a most staunch and loyal supporter of the purple, not to say a fanatic. This is rank heresy and treason."

"You ought to have been in Teddy's lecture this morning," the other inter-rupted, "though it was really no worse than usual. Why, half the class know absolutely nothing about his subject, and never will."

"Among whom we might men-tion?——"

"Yes, I know that, and it's just what makes me sore on myself."

Bigelow laughed. "Really," he began, "I don't see as there will be any objection to your finding out what Teddy is lecturing about, if you choose. They say it can be done, and while it's not the customary thing to worry one's self about such matters, there's nothing criminal in it."

"Come, Dudley, don't give me any more of that sort of stuff. I'm tired of it. Everywhere around college you hear fellows talking about the courses they are taking, as if they were the only things of no importance here. It's the fashion to pretend not to know anything about what you are supposed to be studying. With some of the fellows I admit it's no pretense, but I don't see that that's anything for them to be proud of. With such a fellow as you it's a damned affectation, and it makes me sick. Seriously, what do you think a man comes to college for if not to study and make the most of his opportunities for study?"

Bigelow winced a little at his friend's frankness, but he did not allow his manner to be ruffled at all by it.

"Capital, Bob," he said, laughing. "You will outdo in zeal Hedges the Holy, if you keep on. But, seriously, I think that is just what a man does come here for, if he has a taste for it. It's really a good opportunity to get an education, and I'm patriotic enough to think one can't get a better anywhere in the country than just here."

"Then why do you talk that way?" demanded Bob.

"To be frank with you, my dear boy, I suppose it is because I am just enough of an ass to do so, for the simple reason that the rest do. But that's neither here nor there. As I was saying, if a man has a taste for study let him grind, within moderation, as hard as he pleases. If he hasn't such a taste, and would rather put his energy into athletics, let him devote such a part of his time to the curriculum as he can spare — enough of course to get through — and enjoy life for the rest of it. He will get a bowing acquaintance, at least, with the humanities, which is worth something, and he can't help being influenced for the good by personal contact day after day with men of intellect and scholarly attainments."

"By which you mean, I suppose, that if a man is unfortunate enough to be a blockhead the best thing he can do is to stay here, in the hope that he may by chance absorb something," suggested Bob.

"That's partially it," Bigelow answered coolly. "The fact is that whether a man is a dunce or an intellectual prodigy, the best thing he gets or can get from his college course is not what he learns from books. They have their worth — and great worth, too — but the thing that counts the most is the life here as a whole. That's a very trite observation. You hear it from everybody — but it's true, I think, notwithstanding."

"I think you're wrong, Dud," Bob answered slowly. "I know you hear it everywhere, but I think it's generally from fellows too lazy to work. It seems to me if a fellow can't learn, or won't try, he's no business to be here. He'd better get out and sell

245

beans behind a counter, or do something else that he can make a success
of — and what is more, I think I shall
put my theory into practice before
long," he added, with a short unpleasant laugh.

Bigelow sat up quickly. His room-
mate's decisive tone made him think,
for the first time, that something serious was wrong. Bigelow was a year
ahead of Spaulding, and this advantage, together with a certain alertness
of mind and wider experience, gave
him an influence over his friend that
was not slight. But he knew that if
Bob once made up his mind to a thing,
there was no moving him.

"You'd be very foolish to go now,
Bob," he said earnestly. "It's only
one year more, and the letters themselves are worth something. If you

want to believe that you have wasted
time and opportunities by not paying
more attention to the curriculum, believe it. Perhaps you have In that
case go ahead and grind for the rest
of your course. But, to tell you the
truth, in spite of wasted opportunities
and all that, I don't know a man whom
college has done more for than yourself. It has changed you completely.
You can't realize it yourself, perhaps,
but you are not the same sort of fellow you were when you came here
three years ago."

Bob jumped up from his chair and
began walking up and down the room.
" I know I'm not — I realize that quite
as well as anybody — better, perhaps,"
he added a little bitterly. " I've got a
lot of damn silly notions in my head,
for one thing, that I didn't have when

I came here, and a good many lazy
habits for another, and a great dis-
inclination, besides, to fill the position in life I've been booked for. You
know about what my case is. I am
an only child, and father and mother
thought it would be a good stunt to
send me to college. They didn't have
any particular purpose in view for me,
nor I for myself, but they could afford
it easily enough, and they thought, in
their ignorance, that it would make
more of a man of me. Consequently,
here I am."

Bigelow watched his friend nar-
rowly. Bob was evidently deeply
moved, and Bigelow thought he perceived a specific cause for his dissatis-
faction with himself under the general
reasons he had given. At any rate, it
was not the fact Spaulding had found

248

out that he was failing to learn as much Latin and Math. as some of his classmates, or that he was frittering away his time in idleness, that made him think of leaving the place. That was more or less of a pretext. The truth was, he had suddenly come to the realization of the fact that the influences he had come under at college had been drawing him further and further away from the old life to which he was doubly pledged; and this, he felt, was treason. Whether there was anything more definite than this it was certain Bob's pride would not let him disclose.

Bigelow could see that it would be foolish for him to try to dispossess Bob now of the idea that college was causing a breach between him and the old associations. The only thing was to frankly admit this to be true, and then overrule the objection with considerations of more weight. It was a risky thing to do, but he decided to try it. Bigelow was conscious of the influence he had always had over Bob — an influence due primarily, perhaps, to the fact that he had broader, more mature, and, as a general rule, more correct views on most subjects than his friend; but quite as much because he always asserted them with a cool indifferent sort of superiority which causes conviction of itself.

"College has made you more of a man, Bob," he said, decisively. "And I think you will acknowledge it if you reflect. It has given you new ideas, which you are pleased to call 'damn silly notions,' though you really don't

250

believe them silly notions; it has refined your tastes, developed your character, and given you a broader and
more sympathetic view of men and
things. And what did you come to
college for if not that very thing?"

Spaulding preferred looking uncon-
vinced to any more direct response.

Bigelow continued: "When you
came here — if you pardon me for saying it — you were nothing but a green
village lad. Up to that time you had
only a very narrow circle of associates,
all of them with more or less the same
interests. You came here, and for
three years you have mixed with fellows of all sorts and conditions, rich
and poor, gawky farmer boys, and
fellows who have every social advantage, gospel sharks and dead game
sports; in fact, men of every station

in life, with aims as diverse as the cut of their clothes, and what is more, you have associated with them on terms of an intimacy, which — without any great experience in the world — I should say, was only possible in such a genuine democracy as the American college."

" Oh damn your democracies," Bob muttered.

" This has naturally changed you," Bigelow pursued calmly, " and you must admit the change was for the better, even though it carries with it some discomfort to yourself and others. But, at any rate, it is irremediable. If you think that, by any possible means, you could leave college and revert to the country boy stage, you are mistaken. That's out of the question. The damage is done, if such it be, and the only thing to do is to make the best of it."

Bob got up and put on his hat.

"Perhaps you're right, Dudley," he said. "I'm going to dinner now, anyway."

But in his heart he did not think Bigelow was right. As much as Bob admired his friend, as much as he acknowledged his superiority, as he would have called it, he was by no means blind to his shortcomings. He felt, instinctively, that if Dudley had to choose between his loyalty to another and the culture he made his god, the former would be sacrificed.

Bob went to dinner, and then after an hour spent smoking and reading the newspaper in a friend's room, he strolled over to his German quiz in Hopkins. Not having made any preparation for the quiz, he flunked it cold, the process taking ten minutes in all. "What the deuce is a man like me doing at college anyhow?" he thought. "The best thing I can do is to clear out of here as soon as possible."

He spent another hour or so loafing about doing nothing, and then went down to base ball practice for the want of something better to do.

There he met Caverly Harper. Whatever else Caverly might neglect, he never missed a practice when he was in town; and almost every afternoon he was to be found on the field ready to criticize the team collectively and individually, and the management as well, for the benefit of any one who would listen to him.

"Hello, Robbie," Caverly called out. "What makes you so glum to-day?"

"I flunked my German exam. just now, for one thing," Bob answered, rather absent-mindedly.

Harper evidently considered this a subterfuge, and one that was transparent enough to be taken as a hint that further remark on the subject would be out of order, so he turned the conversation on other topics.

"What do you think of the new freshman pitcher?" he asked. "Hardly varsity material yet, in my opinion — doesn't watch the bases very well. They never do, any of them, when they begin."

They stayed on the field until practice was over, and then strolled uptown together.

"Going to the show in Ad to-night, Bob?" Caverly asked on the way.

"What is it?"

255

"English opera — Robin Hood, I think. I don't know the name of the troupe. Bronson and Reg. and I are going to drive over. Better come along and make the fourth."

Bob walked along for a moment in silence.

"I'm afraid I can't, Cav.," he answered. "I've got to go home for a day or two, and I think I'll start to-night on the 8.19."

Bob went to his room and began putting some of his things into his suit case. He decided not to pack his trunk. He could have it sent on after him. It might happen, of course — but it shouldn't happen. He was going to clear out for good, and he resolutely stifled the hope that anything should make it possible for him to change his mind. Yet, the possibility

256

gave him an excuse to let it be understood that he was only going home to spend Sunday, and so avoid explanations and good-byes. He could come back when he had once made the break final and see all the fellows.

It would have been hard to say what brought him to this decision. It was a foolish one enough, for he could just as well have waited a few weeks longer until college closed, and then gone home with the rest, and not returned in the fall. Then he would not have felt like a deserter.

The truth was that he was in a mood for heroic remedies. He felt that a sacrifice was needed on his part to atone for his implicit disloyalty toward the girl he had promised to marry. The remembrance of their silent misunderstandings, too intangible to be

257

set aright, try as he would, returned to
him again and again like an accusation
against his honor. It was his fault,
not her's. She was the same as when
the romance of their boy and girl love
was everthing to both of them. It
was he that had changed. College,
and the association with his betters,
had made a fool of him. He stuck to
this resolutely. Yet, somehow he
blamed her for not having perceived
the change in him, and resented it
openly. She lacked the fineness of
perception or the pride that a girl
should have. It was this conflict of
mind, in itself degrading, that forced
him to take some action immediately,
that would be final and decisive.

He went to supper purposely late, so
as not to meet the fellows at his table.
When he got back, Bigelow had not

yet come down from his fraternity
house. Bob waited for him awhile,
and then, remembering that he had
not called for his mail since supper,
he started for the Post Office.

Under the trees near West a half a
dozen of his classmates were crowded
on a single settee, smoking and talking. They called to him to come and
join them, but he made some excuse
and went on. In front of Morgan the
usual crowd was playing ball, and from
one of the windows of the dormitory
came the familiar strains of an old college troll, with the tinkling accompani-
ment of the ever-present mandolin.
The streets were full of men in négligé, with tennis rackets under their
arms, or perhaps strolling hither and
thither in sheer idleness.

How foreign to him it all felt. Ex-

cept for the familiar faces everywhere
it was as if he had come back to the
place after years of absence. Then it
struck Bob that it would be harder to
leave college than he had imagined;
and he realized how much it all meant
to him. What a void there would be
in his life when the whole of it should
be a thing of the past.

Bob found a letter from Margery at
the Post Office. He took it from his
box with a feeling of irritation and
walked half way back to Main street,
carrying it in his hand. At last he
broke the seal and began reading
indifferently.

He was totally unprepared for what
he found in the letter. Margery asked
that their engagement should be
broken.

At first he could not suppress a

260

feeling of pleasure, that his release gave him. But the humiliation of the position was not slow to make itself felt. A few words in the letter cut him keenly. "I could see, Bob," she wrote, "that you did not care for me as you thought you did once. I tried not to believe it at first, but I had to in the end. Perhaps it is natural that it should happen so. I do not blame you for I know you were going to act honorably, and keep your promise as well as you could."

Bob's self-contempt was tinged a little, perhaps, with a sort of regret. At any rate it was all over now. He might as well stay at college and make the most of his good time.

Just then Caverly Harper drove by in a double phæton with the two other fellows.   He stopped his horses when he saw Bob.

"We've got lots of room for you," he cried, "if you'll change your mind and go with us."

Bob hesitated a moment.   It seemed as if, in some way, the moment was sacred.   Then he laughed at himself for the idea.

"All right," he cried, "I'm with you."   He stuffed the letter into his pocket and climbed into the phæton, wondering whether college had made a cad of him.

THE NEXT MORNING

263

The Next Morning.

THORNTON came out of the chapel and started toward Hopkins. There was a weariness in his body and a sour taste in his mouth, and the fresh beauty of the morning hurt him like a reproach. Some one called out to him jokingly, " I hear you were in Ad. last night, Bob!" and he laughed back, as a man laughs when he must.

He had plenty of cuts left, for it was early in the term, and, when half way to the recitation, changed his mind and turned up Main street, without any very definite idea of where he was going. He wanted to get away from

265

everybody for awhile and think the thing over.

Twenty minutes' walking carried him well out of the town, almost to the top of Stone Hill, and looking down he could see the college, lying there in the valley, shut in by its circle of hills. The fellows were passing in the street; he almost recognized some of them; the outlines of the buildings stood out sharply against the background of the mountains, and, as he looked, the boom of the Gym. clock came to him through the soft spring air. No Williams man ever forgets that chime.

He half smiled as he remembered how different it had looked to him when he came up from school to take his entrance exams. Then college was a long-desired goal, soon to be attained; an enchanted country inhabi-

266

ted by a privileged race of beings. Even a freshman commanded respect in those days, and a Gargoyle pin was the summit of all earthly wishes.

And now — but he laughed at the idea of comparing himself with that green boy.

The four years had done much for him; they had improved his manners, taught him how to wear his clothes as if they belonged to him, and given him self-confidence and poise. He had made what is called "a success of college," but somehow that morning he didn't seem to care much for any of the offices in the formidable list that followed his name in the last Gul.; even the Gargoyle seemed of comparatively little importance, now that he was in it, and about the only thing he really valued was his class day election as pipe orator, because that showed that the fellows liked him.

He did not particularly regret the events of the night before; he knew that his present gloomy frame of mind was caused quite as much by headache as by the prickings of conscience, and after all, he wasn't sure that he had done anything to be ashamed of. To the undergraduate, drunkenness, unless habitual, is a very venial sin, and there really seemed no need of being so exceedingly remorseful over what he himself would have readily condoned in another.

What troubled him was, to use a colloquialism, "the whole game;" he was not quite sure that his college course hadn't been a failure in spite of its apparent success. He thought of men he knew in the class; men without either his money, or associations, or ability ; men to whom college meant a host of daily sacrifices and mortifications ; to whom life was a serious matter, and self-improvement the end and aim of it. If he had lived as they did would he not now be infinitely better than he was?

But in his heart he knew that he would not change with one of them for worlds. Men admired them in a way, but, after all, they were pitifully ineffective outside of class-room and prayer-meetings. Granted that they were good Christians, they seemed for the most part narrow and intolerant ; and if they were excellent characters, they were also exceedingly tiresome companions. Faugh! The whole tribe disgusted him, as he thought of them, with their serious faces and their flabby muscles. If this were virtue he wanted none of it.

Yet these men were, in a way, his superiors; they were unselfish, earnest and sincere; he felt ashamed to think how many times he had sneered at them. But their life was not his life, and their virtue repelled him. He had great respect for their principles, but he found them uninteresting as friends; and their religion had always seemed to him just a little bit pharisaical.

And, after all, were they more virtuous than he, or only more scrupulous? He had his principles as well as they, and kept them, for the most part, quite as carefully. He was loyal to his friends, and told the truth on all occasions. If he sometimes indulged in a *risque* story, or drank a little too much, as he had done last night, he was, on the whole, neither foul-minded nor intemperate. He was simply "one of the crowd," an average college man, with the usual vices and virtues, mingled in about the usual proportions.

No, he was better than that. He did not do many things that most people took as a matter of course. There were stories he would not tell, and jokes that he would not laugh at, and more than once he had risked unpopularity when some one had spoken slightingly of a girl in a room full of men.

But he felt that he had lost something in those four years, or rather that it had been taken away from him. It is impossible for a man to go through college without getting, as people say, "a knowledge of the world," which phrase also includes a knowledge of the flesh and the devil; even if we fight against evil the contact soils us, and Thornton had not always fought.

He had come to college straight from home, younger in many ways than most of the men in his class. His virtue was the virtue that his mother had taught him as a little boy, and though he was not prudish, nor a fool, he was innocent and pure. It hurt him to think how he had changed since then; how, one by one, he had lost his ideals and abandoned his principles, until now he had scarcely anything left except his honesty and his chivalry.

Yet he knew that he had fared better than many, and that his former innocence was founded quite as much upon ignorance as upon virtue. It had been all very well for the boy, but it would have looked a little out of place in the

272

man; one cannot be too particular if one wishes to be effective.

And he was effective. He knew it and rejoiced in the thought. He was a force in college; his opinion was sought and his example followed, and probably he did quite as much good as the most pious Y. M. C. A. man with all his self-conscious religion. But he flushed a little when he thought how he must have appeared last night, with his stained, disordered clothes, and his foolish, maudlin conversation. No, he had wasted his time and misused his opportunities; if he was not positively bad, he was certainly weak, and weakness was worse than vice.

He thought of Jack Thompson and felt ashamed of himself. Jack was in the Gargoyle, too, and had played foot

273

ball four years, and won the Clark scholarship besides. No one ever called him a Y. M. C. A. shark, and no one ever told a doubtful story when he was in the room.

Jack led the class prayer-meetings and the cheering at Amherst with equal enthusiasm. He was going to be a medical missionary in some out of the way place with a bloodthirsty population and an unhealthy climate. Thornton admired a man like that thoroughly; he wished he knew him better, and it surprised him a little that, in spite of his admiration, he had never made any serious attempt to become intimate with Jack Thompson. Perhaps if he had ——

"Shay, old feller, isn't thish the way ter Williamstown?"

He looked up quickly. The speaker

was a man of about thirty, dressed in overalls and a loose flannel shirt, and evidently very, very drunk. Thornton smiled a little.

"I suppose I should take you for a moral lesson, my friend," he said, half aloud, "but why did you select this unusually early hour for your little indulgences?"

"Wha'sh that?" said the individual, thickly; "isn't thish the way ter Williamstown?"

"I beg your pardon," answered Thornton, "I was merely thinking aloud; most impolite of me, I am sure. Yes, this is the way to Williamstown."

"There!" exclaimed the other, triumphantly, "I knew it were! Some damn fool back on the road told me it weren't, but I knew it were; yes," he repeated, after a long and thoughtful pause, " I knew it were."

" My dear sir," replied Thornton, gravely, "you are indeed fortunate. After having spent three hours a week for many months in discussing the question, ' What is it to know?' I am rejoiced to find one who has solved the problem. Let me congratulate you."

" Tha'sh true," said he of the overalls, obscurely, but heartily, " tha'sh true. Shay," he continued, confidentially, " ye'r an awful nice feller."

" Thank you," answered Thornton.

" Yesh ye are," said the man, coming nearer, "and I'm goin' ter stay and talk ter-ye-while," and he lurched down on the grass and threw one arm around the other's neck.

" Really," said Thornton, a little

startled, "this affection is very touching, but it would be rather embarrassing if any one should see us, and I really think I'll have to be walking on."

"Tha'sh right," answered the man, staggering to his feet, "we'll both go down tergether and tell the sup'rintendent how it was."

Here was a new development; evidently he was not going home. Thornton felt curious. "What superintendent do you mean?" he asked.

"Why, the one at the Bleachery," replied the man, indignantly; "what one did ye think I meant? Why, I work down there, didn't ye know that? I thought ye was a nice feller!"

"I'm afraid I'm shamefully ignorant," answered Thornton.

"Well," said the man, "I'll tell ye

277

'bout it. Ye see, the sup'rintendent, he sez ter me last month, 'Doyle,' sez he, tha'sh me, 'if ye come here drunk again I'll discharge ye.' 'All right,' sez I, 'wait till I do;' and I ain't been drunk since, and I ain't goin' ter be; and I'm goin' right down there now, and if the sup'rintendent starts ter shay an'thing, do ye know what I'm goin' ter do?" He paused and sunk his voice into a hoarse whisper; "I'm goin' ter knock him down;" he finished impressively.

Thornton laughed, and started on up the road, then changed his mind and came back again. "Look here!" he said, "don't you want to take a walk with me?"

"No," answered the other, suspiciously; "No, ye think I'm drunk and I ain't; and ye ain't no business

to think I'm drunk when I ain't; I'm
goin' ter see the sup'rintendent."

"Of course you are," said Thornton,
soothingly, "we'll go together." He
locked arms with him, and, by means
of persistent pulling and constant talking, finally got him to come with him
with no more active opposition than
an occasional "Shay, w'ere we goin'
ter?" which he answered by a con-
fident "That's all right, we're going
to see the superintendent."

Thornton led his charge across the
fields, having considerable trouble with
the fences, and at last arrived at the
brook that runs to the west of Stone
Hill. He walked along the bank until
they came to a pretty deep place, and
then picked the man bodily off his
feet, and, without further ceremony,
tumbled him in. It was pretty heroic

279

treatment, for the water was almost ice cold, but it was the only quick and sure method available of sobering him, and Thornton resolved to risk the chance of giving him pneumonia.

There was a great deal of splashing and sputtering, considerable bad language, and a very wet and dazed look ing man crawled out of the brook and stared round about him confusedly.

Thornton took him by the shoulder. "Look here," he said, "pull yourself together and listen to me. May be you don't remember meeting me up on the road and talking nonsense about assaulting people. Listen," he repeated, roughly, "you were drunk. Do you understand? Dead, rotten, foolish drunk, and you were going down to the Bleachery to lick the superintendent. You'd have been discharged if I hadn't brought you here and thrown you into the brook to sober you up? Can you hear me? To sober you up;" and he assisted the sobering process by shaking the man until his teeth rattled like castanets, and he raised his hand protestingly.

"Quit," he said, weakly, "quit, will ye; I'm not drunk now."

Thornton let go of him and he sank limply down on the grass and stayed there, half sitting and half lying down, while his scattered faculties came back to him. Finally, he got up on his feet and pushed the wet hair uncertainly from his face.

"Drunk, was I?" said he, slowly. "Well, I guess I was. What did I say ter ye, anyway?"

Thornton told him again, and the man looked at him with a gradually growing comprehension of the situation.

"So I was goin' ter lick the superintendent?" he asked, at length, "and ye kept me from gettin' fired. What a damn fool I was." He stopped a minute; then his face lighted up with a new idea, and he held out his hand. "Shake," he said, awkwardly.

"O, that's all right," said Thornton, shaking hands with him; "now, you'd better get home as fast as you can. You don't want to have a chill, you know."

"That's so," he answered. "Well, good day to ye, and thank ye again." He turned to go and then faced around suddenly. "Say," he exclaimed, "ye'r a damn good feller."

"Never mind that now," said Thornton, "run home, or you'll catch cold."

The Next Morning.

But the man was thinking of something else.

"Yes," he repeated, "ye'r a damn good feller; ye didn't try any preachin', and ye acted like ye knew just how I was feelin' and wasn't disgusted, ner helpin' me becuz ye thought ye ought ter. Say," he continued, almost timidly, "'scuse me fer askin' it, but ye seem different from most of 'em. Beg yer pardin, but ain't ye been drunk yerself?"

Thornton winced. "Yes," he answered, slowly, "yes, I've been drunk myself."

IN HONOR OF THE SAINT

In Honor of the Saint.

"' But what good came of it at last?'
  Quoth little Peterkin,
 ' Why, that I cannot tell,' said he,
 ' But 'twas a famous victory.'"

IT all happened because the fresh-
    man class was so very fresh. Of
course all freshman classes are fresh,
otherwise what fun would there be for
the sophomores fall term; but that
year it was unusually so. Some even
said that it was the freshest class that
ever entered college, and one must
admit there was some ground for the
statement. A few men there were, of
a certainty, in it, whose assurance was
apparently unbounded. Take Clarence

Raeburn, for instance, who arrived in town, clad in a pink and green plaid golf suit, with a bundle of canes in one hand and a silk hat case in the other, and succeeded during the first week in making himself so much at home that he called half the upper classmen by their Christian names.

Then there was Fitch, who complacently congratulated Mrs. Harding, at the President's reception, on the good work her husband, Prof. Harding, was doing in his freshman French course,—the President's reception is a famous place for *mauvais mots;* and Pritchard, who made the well-intended but ineffectual attempt to lead the cheering at the first foot ball game on Weston Field; not to mention Kendall, who attended the dance at the Greylock, and little Witherbee, with his silly

notions about the right of a free-born
man, even if he be a freshman, to do
what he pleases. These are a few
shining examples, but there were many
more like them.

Indeed, Clyde Hamilton himself
was decidedly fresh, and to this
quality he owed beyond question
something of the popularity which
had secured him his election as
speaker for the freshmen in the Shirt
Tail parade celebration; and in consequence the misfortunes which befell
him on that memorable day.

Clyde, from the time he entered college, had taken a prominent position
among the freshmen, a position which
was strengthened, rather than the reverse, by the attention, not entirely
flattering, which he received from the
classes above his own. As it hap-

pened, he was one of the trio at the sophomore-freshman base ball game who were made to stand on the scorer's table and sing "Three Little Maids from School" before a coach load of visitors from out of town. But considerably before this the sophomores had marked his lack of proper freshman-like humility of manner, and had already made one or two friendly calls upon him in his room in Morgan, at which the host was asked repeatedly to give evidence of his vocal and declamatory powers. During these little informal at homes Clyde was always very affable and obliging, complying gracefully to the requests of his guests,— and afterward was as imperturbably fresh as ever.

All this gained him considerable notice among his classmates, and when the time came to elect the St. Patrick's Day orator, Clyde was chosen to the office unanimously and with great enthusiasm.

Every one said the parade that year would be a great success on account of the warmth of feeling between the lower classes; or at least that there would be plenty of fun of one sort or other, for the sophomores had vowed, that, as far as the procession itself was concerned, it should be a most dismal failure if there was muscle enough in the sophomore class to break it up. On the other hand, the freshmen, who were spending no end of time and money on fireworks and transparencies and so forth, resolved to do their best to give their opponents a warm reception if they should make any such attempt; and as the upper classmen were supposed to be on the side of peace, they hoped to get down to the campus in good order.

The first skirmish occurred on the eve of St. Patrick's Day, and its termination greatly elated the freshmen. The sophs, of course, had been on the lookout for the freshman canes for several days, and when some one discovered that a box had come to the express office that morning from Troy, addressed to the chairman of the cane committee, they decided at once to capture it at any cost. During the whole day some of them hung about the express office, but no one appeared to claim the box. At last, however, a little after six o'clock, twelve or fifteen of the biggest men in the freshmen class collected at the office, got out the box and carried it up the hill toward the Labs., all bunched together ready to repel any attack.

Fred Hillis, the football player, was on guard for the sophomores.

"Canes! Canes! Freshman canes," he shouted, and in a moment there were thirty or forty sophs pushing and struggling to wrest the box away from the freshmen. Both sides fought valiantly, and for a time neither got the advantage. But finally a sophomore jumped into the bunch of freshmen, and landing on the box, knocked it out of their hands. The freshmen tried to pick it up again, but their adversaries were getting the advantage.

" Break it open," shouted one of the sophs. Some one gave it a great kick and the top was broken in. In a moment the sophomores had torn off the boards. Within they found stones and shavings instead of the canes.

"Rubber, rubber," shouted the freshmen, and took to their heels.

One can imagine this did not serve to cool the feeling between the two classes. Neither did the jeering of the freshmen all that evening; nor the sheet with the mystic words "Rubber Neck," and the numerals of the sophomore class painted upon it, which was seen nailed on the cupola of West the next morning.

But the sophomores did not allow their chagrin to show itself outwardly. During the day all was quiet with the calm that comes before the storm, for every one was predicting excitement when evening should come. The leading sophomores cut recitations and stood about vaguely in groups, saying

little, but looking very important and
ominous.

However, there were some who
were not to be satisfied by promising
themselves the pleasure of smashing
transparencies and rolling freshmen in
the mud, if they could, that evening.
They planned a sweeter and a surer
revenge. Fred Hillis was at the bottom of it.

"We'll fix that damn freshman," he
exclaimed to the two or three chosen
conspirators. "I'll bet his nerve will
wilt this time."

One of them roomed in the west
entry of Morgan, on the ground floor,
and they all waited there during the
whole afternoon, with the door open a
crack and somebody on guard.

At six o'clock Clyde Hamilton, who
lived on the floor above, came down

to go to supper. Just as he got to the bottom of the stairs four or five men rushed out on him. Hamilton was a good-sized fellow, but his struggles were useless, and, in a moment, before he could recognize his assailants, he was blindfolded, dragged a little way and bound down on a bed, gagged with a handkerchief.

"There, think over your sins, freshman," some one said, and then they all went out laughing, and Clyde heard the door locked after them.

Clyde, being a practical fellow, did not employ himself as the sophomore suggested, but began trying to get free. It was useless. He was bound hand and foot, and, wriggle and squirm as he would, there was no escape.

Pretty soon his captors returned, bringing some other fellows with them.

The bedroom door was opened, and he had the pleasant consciousness that he was being shown to the newcomers.

"I fear Clyde's mellifluous voice will not be heard on the campus to-night," some one remarked jocosely.

"I fear not; but how quiet he lies," said another; "I believe he's asleep."

"Sleep while you can, little one," cried a third; "good friends watch over thee."

This was decidedly unpleasant for Clyde, who felt himself redden hotly. He recognized some of the voices, and made one or two very foolish vows which circumstances, fortunately, absolved him from keeping.

Presently the bedroom door was closed, and he heard the crowd out in the study discussing plans for the attack on the parade.

"Well I'm going to my room and put on a sweater," some one said after a while, and then he knew that the fun was about to begin.

The party dropped off one by one, and at last the door was closed and locked again. Clyde heard the fellows all coming down stairs, laughing and talking. Some of them he recognized as his classmates. He struggled again to loosen his bonds but without result.

It was hard luck to have to lie there and let the show go on without him, and especially hard, as Clyde had been planning all along to make the hit of the evening. How those sophs would jolly him about it, and the Gul. too. He thought of the speech he had prepared with such an expenditure of time and energy. Wasn't he going to roast those sophs, though? Not openly, of course, but covertly, with delicate irony, and biting innuendo, cleverly concealed under the modest language which it beseems a freshman to use. There were some in the upper classes also whom he would score, still more artfully. Yes, certainly his speech would have been the feature of the celebration.

By this time Morgan was empty of its occupants and silent as the tomb. Clyde listened an intolerable time without hearing any noise. Then very faintly came the sound of music. The procession was forming and he was not there.

Of course his absence had been discovered by this time, and great had been the lamentation among the freshmen. Every one asked every one else who had seen him last, but nothing definite could be learned. The sophs had abducted him, that was sure; but it was too late to make any search, and some one else had to be chosen to fill his place. This made a great deal of confusion. No one wanted the office under the circumstances, and everybody had some one else who was particularly fitted for it.

Caverly Harper, who was on the committee of arrangements from the upper classes, finally settled the matter by pulling Raeburn out of the anxious, white-robed crowd.

"You'll do," he cried. "You've got crust enough for anything. Pull off your shirt," and he forthwith lifted the unwilling orator-to-be into the wagon.

In Honor of the Saint.

By this time little freshman Pingree was also divested of his white garment and was running up Main street as fast as his legs could carry him. Little Pingree, despite his simplicity of manner, had that very rare faculty, the ability of putting two and two together in a hurry. If the sophs have captured Hamilton, he thought, they have probably locked him up in one of their rooms and left him to go out and see the parade. Pingree was of a poetic and imaginative nature, and he recollected very vividly of reading in a Sunday school book, a long time ago, how Blondel went around through Germany, singing under castle walls, until at last he discovered where his royal pupil was immured. Perhaps Hamilton might yet make his speech and throw the enemy into confusion. At any rate it was worth while making the attempt. He decided to try Morgan first. That was the most likely place.

To avoid the sophomores, he had to go away back of Griffin and around by the Hash House and Hopkins. He began in Hell's Entry, giving his class cheer distinctly, but softly, on each landing. There was no response. Apparently the rooms were empty. He went on to the next staircase, and then to the next, but still no answer came. He had thrown off all fear now and was shouting at the top of his voice. By the time he had reached the west entry he was beginning to be discouraged. On the ground floor he yelled twice and then cried, "Oh, Hamilton!" but without result. Then, when he was half way up the first flight, he heard a muffled cry from one of the rooms.

"Let me out for Heaven's sake," some one said.

"Is that you, Hamilton?" Pingree exclaimed, almost tumbling down stairs in his excitement.

"Yes, it is; smash the door in and untie me."

Pingree threw himself against the door, but it did not give.

"I'll go outside, and come in through the window," he said breathlessly, after three or four more futile attempts.

The streets were crowded now and it was a risky business, but no one apparently heard the sound of the breaking glass, and in a moment Pingree had unfastened the latch, pulled up the sash and climbed in.

"They had me gagged," Hamilton

explained, "but when I heard you shout I managed to get the handkerchief out of my mouth."

"Oh, those Cobleighs," sighed Pingree, plaintively, working away at the knots; "I knew they had got a hold of you."

In a moment Hamilton was freed. "The procession will be down the street in a moment," Pingree explained; "you can go out and get into the wagon as it comes along,"

"No," said Clyde, thoughtfully; "we may as well do the thing up dramatically. We'll give the sophs a little surprise just in the nick of time. Besides, I've not had any supper, and I'm hungry. This is Ted's room, and I know the ropes here," he added, lighting a match and making for the closet.

He returned in a moment with a box of crackers. After finishing with these he groped about and finally found a pipe and filled it, stretching himself out comfortably on the divan. Clyde liked to do things of this sort, especially when there was somebody like Pingree around to look on in admiration. It was almost as good as being one of Mr. Anthony Hope's characters.

"You go on, old man, if you want to," he said to Pingree, after a few puffs, "and see the sport. I'll be there all in good time."

But, of course, Pingree would hear of no such thing, and so the two sat there in the dark talking in low voices.

Meanwhile the parade had formed down by the Methodist church, and proceeded up Main street to the strains of " Come fill your glasses up," rendered in an uncertain manner by the Williamstown band, which headed the procession. Next to the band came the wagon containing the committee of upper classmen and the three speakers of the evening. Then two by two, in a long column, marched the freshmen, all clad in their white attire and carrying torches and Roman candles. Here and there along the line were large muslin transparencies uplifted on poles, on which were chronicled in terse and telling phrases such events in the history of sophomore-freshmen interrelations as the freshmen desired to blazon before the world. The largest and most conspicuous bore a rough representation of a box, and under it the single word "Rubber" in gigantic characters. Around these transparencies the strongest men in the class were placed, for they were sure to be points of attack. Up through the mud they splashed, while along beside them on the sidewalks and grass plots walked the upper classmen, to see the fun and act as a guard against sophomore attack.

The streets were crowded. Small boys, gray-whiskered farmers and factory hands from North Adams and Blackinton jostled each other noisily but good naturedly. The younger element of the faculty was also well represented.

Just at the top of Consumption Hill, around the Soldiers' Monument, the scene of many a hard-contested rush in the good old days of monument rushing, were congregated the sophomores, eager and determined. When the first transparency appeared

over the brow of the hill they gave a
great shout and rushed at it in a body.
The freshmen stood their ground valiantly, and the juniors and seniors ran
to their aid, only too glad to taste
again the joys of their underclass-
man days. But the sophomores were
bunched and not to be resisted. The
white line wavered, then broke ; white
and black figures rolled in the mud
together, torches were extinguished,
and Roman candles discharged themselves in the wildest riot. In a
moment, more of the upper classmen
arrived at the theatre of war, and the
sophomores were forced back and
the line of march reformed. But of
the transparency only a sad wreck
remained.

Again and again the same sort of
attack was made, always with the re-

sult of smashing transparencies and temporarily throwing into confusion the paraders, who, however, formed themselves into line again and proceeded on their march to the tune of the patient band, muddy and bedraggled but persistent.

Up Main street they went, around the park and then down to the Gym. Here ranks were broken and a disordered rush of all classes for the old campus ensued. In the middle of the field the great heap of boxes and barrels was beginning to blaze. The band arrived playing a fast and furious two step, and in a moment the freshmen were circling around the fire hand in hand. The flames leaped high into the sky, revealing in a ruddy light the mass of faces up on the slopes to the north and east, which, with the hundred white-clad, dancing figures below made the place look like the pit of Malebolge in the Inferno.

The freshmen had hardly formed their circle when the rush for the shirts began. Almost instantly every freshman was divested of his garment by some eager sophomore. But that did not end the matter. Every one now tried to get and keep as many torn shreds of the shirts as he could. The struggle lasted for five minutes and was carried on on all parts of the field. Generally it was between a single sophomore and freshman, but sometimes there would be a half a dozen contestants pulling and straining at one little bit of muddy cloth. Finally time was called, the music was hushed, and every one crowded about the wagon to hear the speeches.

In Honor of the Saint.

Shirt Tail Parade oratory does not have to be of a polished, Ciceronian sort. Provided it is fairly witty and personal, nothing further is required. In these respects Thornton's speech was a success. He touched lightly upon the peculiarities of some of the sophomores, gave some fatherly advice to the freshmen, indulged in a few sarcasms at the expense of the faculty,— whose weaknesses are fortunately always with us for the purpose of ridicule — and then, introducing the speaker for the sophomore class, sat down amid the usual applause.

Ned Allerton then arose from his seat in the wagon. "Ladies and gentlemen and freshmen," he began, "I confess that I accepted my election to this office with considerable hesitation. The prospect of riding in the same

311

wagon with such a distinguished person as Mr. Clyde Hamilton was, of itself, enough to disconcert a man far more self-possessed than I. But, besides that, I knew that his powers of oratory would put mine completely in the shade, and I am sure that those of my class who have heard Mr. Hamilton speak on less public occasions than this, will bear me out in the statement. But I have been informed that, for some unaccountable reason, probably best known to himself, Mr. Hamilton has decided not to address you to-night; and while I grieve that we are not to be favored with an exhibition of such eloquence as he would undoubtedly give us, I cannot but feel relieved, for my own sake, and consequently approach my task with less embarrassment." The speaker paused amid the cheering of his classmates, and then began the speech he had prepared.

When he had finished, Thornton got up to introduce the freshman speaker. " Ladies and gentlemen," he said, "it would be useless for me to make any comment upon the statement which the last gentleman made, concerning the unexpected absence of Mr. Clyde Hamilton. I wish simply to introduce to you " — here Thornton's eye fell by chance on somebody standing just below him with his hand on the wagon — " I wish simply to introduce to you," he repeated, after a moment of hesitation, " as the speaker for the freshmen class,— Mr. Clyde Hamilton."

A burst of wild applause came from the freshmen, and in a moment Clyde was standing on the seat of the wagon ready to begin his oration.

In Honor of the Saint.

Whether he made the hit of the evening is a mooted question. The freshmen were enthusiastic in affirming that he did, while, on the other hand, the sophomores were vigorous in their denial of it. But, at any rate, his speech was greatly applauded by those present. When he had finished, the big, wooden hatchet was buried in the glowing embers of the bonfire, and the hostilities between sophomores and freshmen were at an end.

THE END OF THE
BEGINNING

315

The End of the Beginning.

___

'And year by year our memory fades
From all the circle of the hills — "

IN every class, when it comes to be
graduated, there is, in addition to
the number in good and regular standing, who go up to get the sheepskin
reward of their scholarly attainments,
and who afterwards sit in tired importance at the long tables in the Gym.,
eating wilted strawberries and cold
soup, and trying to look like real
alumni,— a " lost legion " of classmates
who wear no black gowns, who are not
addressed by the President, who hear
no class-day speeches, but, falling early
or late along the path of knowledge,

317

are scattered abroad; forgotten, for the most part, after a little, save when the kindly Gul. remembers them, and in its catalogue of the classes, prints a list of their names as "sometime members."

Good fellows these are, for the most part,— the best of good fellows go first somehow — but who had an unfortunate inability to come up to absurdly exacting classical or scientific standards, or, it may be, whose sense of the humor of life exceeded the limits of becoming mirth.

Neither of these, however, was the reason for Teddie Carroll's dropping out of the Best of all Classes at the beginning of his senior year. Typhoid fever, that autumnal terror, had bowled him over, and after his convalescence, while his friends and for-

mer classmates were snow bound up
in the wintry New England hills,
Carroll was slowly creeping back into
life again on the other side of the
world instead of being among them.
It was only an invalid's fancy, perhaps, but often he would have
exchanged the softest and tenderest
of Italian hillsides for a glimpse of
Prospect looming in glistening majesty
against the turquoise of the wintry
sky; or have turned from the Medi-
terranean in its most divine mood
to the shining wastes of snow stretching away to the west on a clear still
afternoon.

Carroll never supposed that he
would miss the place as he did; and
it was only when he was thousands
of miles away from it, that he began
to realize his love for it. But he

came back in the spring, just in time to see his class graduate. "In at the finish," as Worthington Winthrop had said, when he came up to the Greylock to welcome him back the night of his arrival.

"You'll be at chapel in the morning, of course. It's Hi Juvenes, you know," Winthrop said as he bade Carroll's mother good night.

"Hi Juvenes" did not carry any definite impression to Mrs. Carroll's mind, but she smiled and said 'of course—that she meant to go to all the commencement exercises.

At least once a year chapel ceases to be a compulsion and late naps and breakfasts are made a free-will sacrifice. And this is on Hi Juvenes— the last chapel service that the seniors attend as a class. This particular

The End of the Beginning.

June morning seemed made to order for the Best of all Classes,— cool, blue and cloudless, with a light wind to stir the trees and weave the leafy shadows with the sun.

The chapel was nearly full when Teddie came in with his mother: the sophomores, in their seats, trying to show that they had been through it all before; on the opposite side and down into the transept, with the great Garfield window darkling above them, the freshmen — interested, curious and impressed; next to them the juniors, with the shadow of the end just beginning to creep upon them.

"The empty pews are waiting for the seniors, I suppose?" Mrs. Carroll said. Her son nodded. The old habit of thought still remained. He felt out of place back there among all the faculty wives and visitors. Then he remembered that in a moment more his class was to sit there in those waiting, vacant seats for the last time. The place seemed full of flowers,— bowls and jars of them — iris and heavy branches of lilac and early roses, the sort of flowers that the faculty gardens are sweet with. Against the deep colored curtains behind the pulpit the numerals of the class gleamed out in the golden whiteness of syringa flowers; and above them, between the shining pipes of the organ, were masses of the shadowy greenness of wood ferns. Over the sound of the music one could hear the chapel bell ringing the three strokes of the last warning relentlessly. A freshman hurried in and took his seat. The bell, with one final, careless clang, ceased.

The End of the Beginning.

The organ music had almost died away and then, as in response to some signal, swelled out into broad, sweeping harmonies.

"They are coming," Carroll whispered. The sophomores nearest the door had risen, and the others followed their example. Up the aisle, through the lane the standing men made, swept the President, the wide sleeves of his stiff, black silk gown brushing against them as he passed. Then the marshals came, the biting purple of their cap tassels and of their baton ribbons striking a glad note of color against the blackness of their gowns. The rest of the class followed, two by two, swinging slowly behind them, with the organ pealing as if in welcome.

Carroll swallowed hard and his eyes

grew bright,— he had been ill, you
see, and little things affected him.

"Aren't they a splendid crowd?"
he whispered to his mother, under
the confusion that came as the men
looked for their seats. "See, that big
chap over there is Fields, the foot-ball
captain, the man who got the pennant
for Williams last year. And the little
fellow next to him is Reese, who draws
so well. Young? Yes, he does look
it, but he can take care of himself all
right. That's Billy Withers just behind him,— you've heard me speak of
Billy. They say he has gotten engaged,— I must ask him about it.
The tall fellow with the light hair is
Alexander, one of the finest men I
ever knew. That's Holbrook, just sitting down, who won every prize in
sight. And do you see the stocky lit-

tle chap with curly hair and glasses? That's Hardy, the ball player. But I've told you all about him lots of times. Which? The one behind Hardy? Oh, Bob Akerly, the most all round man in college."

Carroll was suddenly forced to stop his cataloging, for the service had begun,—the simple, straightforward, little service, that, somehow, this morning had acquired a new solemnity and beauty. They sang "Ein Feste Burg" at the end, every man of them joining in. Very likely it was the inspiration of the time and the music that gave to the splendid battle song of youth and courage an unaccustomed power and volume. And then a hush and a benediction, and afterwards, with the undergraduates standing to honor them, the Best of all

325

The End of the Beginning.

Classes filed down the aisle and out of the chapel into the early sunshine,—alumni.

They cheered, then, first for Williams, of course, and then for their class, and after that for the other classes as they crowded out and formed into groups, cheering in answer.

The reaction followed, — an anti-climax of good-natured horse play, that came as gratefully, after all the emotional tension of the morning, as the comic relief in a highly wrought play. The others had come out from the building by this time, and stood watching the merry confusion of flying gowns and scurrying men.

Carroll and his mother were standing a little apart from the others. " Dear boy," Mrs. Carroll said, after a little silence, " is it much harder than you thought not to be with them ? " He was looking across the wavering summer greenness to where, far beyond, the hills stood like sentinels on guard.

" I'm sorry, of course, not to have stayed with them to the end," he said slowly, " but, after all, I shall always be a Williams man."